"You win, Leslie. Will you marry me?"

Leslie felt drunk with triumph. Dane had actually proposed! All of her scheming had worked!

"I can't sleep, I can't eat and I can't even look at another woman!" Dane went on. "And if you refuse, I'll make your life hell till you agree!"

"Put like that, how can I say no?" Leslie replied huskily, rethinking herself into the role she had created. "It's just that I find it hard to believe you really love me, Dane."

"But I don't," he announced smoothly. "I desire you, ache for you, and you even have my friendship and respect. But I'm marrying you because I can't have you any other way. Well?"

Suddenly Leslie no longer felt so elated, though it really shouldn't be important to her plan that Dane love her, too.

ROBERTA LEIGH wrote her first book at the age of nineteen and since then has written more than seventy romance novels, as well as many books and film series for children. She has also been an editor of a woman's magazine and produced a teen magazine, but writing romance fiction remains one of her greatest joys. She lives in Hampstead, London, and has one son.

Books by Roberta Leigh

HARLEQUIN PRESENTS

HARLEQUIN ROMANCE

Don't miss any of our special offers. Write to us at the following address for information on our newest releases.

Harlequin Reader Service
901 Fuhrmann Blvd., P.O. Box 1397, Buffalo, NY 14240
Canadian address: P.O. Box 603,
Fort Erie, Ont. L2A 5X3

ROBERTA LEIGH

too bad to be true

Harlequin Books

TORONTO • NEW YORK • LONDON
AMSTERDAM • PARIS • SYDNEY • HAMBURG
STOCKHOLM • ATHENS • TOKYO • MILAN

Harlequin Presents first edition January 1988
ISBN 0-373-11043-X

Original hardcover edition published in 1987
by Mills & Boon Limited

CHAPTER ONE

As Leslie Watson heard the judge deliver the alimony award in her stepfather's divorce case, she couldn't believe her ears. It was so weighted in his ex-wife's favour she had to force herself not to jump up and say so.

Glancing across the Los Angeles courtroom, she saw her stepmother Charlene beam happily at her lawyer, who gave her a faint smile in return. Yet Dane Jordan should be beaming too, for like many American lawyers his fee was on a percentage basis, and he had just earned himself a fortune!

Leslie knew it wasn't the alimony that would worry her stepfather so much as the fact that his ex-wife had been allowed to keep the large block of shares in his company, which he had given her as a wedding gift four years ago. At the time, his friends and family had warned him not to do it; warned him also against marrying a girl thirty years his junior—Charlene was only a few years older than Leslie. But he wouldn't hear a word against the beautiful nurse who had taken care of him after a near-fatal heart attack, and was now paying the price for his obstinacy.

Watching him, Leslie was afraid he would soon have another attack, though he had shown no outward emotion even when Charlene—devoid of make-up to emphasise her youthful innocence—had flung him a triumphant look as the judge announced his decision.

Only as Dane Jordan walked across the court towards him did he show any sign of stress, his features hardening as he ignored the lawyer's out-stretched hand.

'No hard feelings, I hope, Mr Webb,' the younger man said, pretending unawareness of the snub. 'But it's my job to do my best for my client.'

To the exclusion of all else, Leslie thought grimly, Dane Jordan's words fuelling the dislike she had felt for him long before seeing him in action. His ruthless ability had become a legend, making him famous throughout the States, and he was ideal fodder for the news media, for he played as hard as he worked, squiring some of the loveliest girls in a city noted for beautiful women.

Yet though Leslie found little to admire in him as a person, she could not decry his professional brilliance. Like many famous trial lawyers, he was a consummate actor, using his dark good looks and sharp brain to swing the mood of judge and jury.

Wending her way through the crush of newsmen clustering around Charlene, Leslie reached the exit at the same time as her stepfather.

'It was thoughtful of you to come, honey,' he said heavily, putting an affectionate hand on her shoulder. 'I know how busy you are.'

'Never too busy for you,' she said truthfully. 'I only wish I could have given you more than moral support. That Jordan's a ruthless swine!'

'A winning swine—which is what counts.'

'You'll appeal, of course. I'm sure you can make Charlene give you back those shares.'

'I'm willing to *buy* them from her,' came the instant rejoinder. 'If she sells them to Imtex, I'm finished.'

Leslie bit back a sigh. Imtex International had been trying to win control of her stepfather's company for as long as she could remember, and if Charlene sold them her shares, they would be able to do so.

'If you offer her a high enough price I'm sure she'll sell them to you,' Leslie placated.

'That's what I'm counting on.'

They were outside the courthouse, and she headed towards her car. 'How about lunching with me now you're a free man?'

'I'd rather make it dinner. I want to get back to my office and thrash out a few things.'

'Fine,' she agreed, though it really wasn't, for she had a date for tonight. 'I'll book a table at the Bistro.'

It was where Peter Denver was taking her and she hoped he would be understanding enough to give her his reservation. She had been out with him three times and liked him enough not to want to put him off. But her affection for her stepfather outweighed all other considerations.

'You must have a lot of influence if you can get into the Bistro at such short notice,' Robert teased her.

'It's my charm!' she fibbed. 'I'll see you there at eight.'

Reaching her car, Leslie pulled the parking ticket from her windscreen. The third this week, and it was only Tuesday! But with space at a premium, and a good deal of her work centering around Beverly Hills, it was an inconvenience she was able to shrug off, especially as her firm paid the fines—one of the many perks that came from being with a large company.

Driving back to her office, she reflected how lucky she was to be working for Morrissey Associates since qualifying as an architect four years ago. She had turned down a more lucrative offer in New York in order to live near her stepfather, and found her job in California satisfyingly varied. Her distinctive style was already earning her a growing reputation in the state, and one of the directors in her firm had hinted at a partnership before the year's end.

She had Robert Webb to thank for everything, of course. Her natural father had died when she was three, leaving her mother with a heavily mortgaged house and no money. Luckily she had met and married Robert—a middle-aged widower with two teenage sons—soon after, but their happiness had been shortlived, for she had died on their fifth anniversary, leaving her young daughter in his care.

Robert had loved Leslie as if she were his own, and so had his two placid, lanky sons. The only sad thing, she mused, halting at a red light, was that neither of the boys had elected to go into his business; Pete, the older, now a research chemist in Boston, and Dick running a successful art gallery in Santa Fé. Perhaps that was why her stepfather had married Charlene. Friends were no replacement for family, and he must have found life lonely, especially when she herself had been away at college.

The stop sign turned green, and Leslie swung into her parking bay beneath her office building, then took the elevator to the tenth floor.

'How did it go?' her secretary asked as she walked in.

'Couldn't have been worse.' Leslie gave her a summary of the hearing, knowing that tomorrow's papers would be full of the gory details.

'Any messages?' she asked when she had finished.

'Several. All wanting you to call back!'

'OK. But get me Peter Denver first.'

A few minutes later, Leslie was explaining why she was cancelling her date with him. Happily he was understanding, and postponed it to the following evening, then delighted her by offering her his table for tonight.

He really was the nicest of her boy-friends, she thought as she hung up, and wished she were less nervous when it came to a commitment. But still, with a blossoming career she had every right to be wary. Marriage might start out with both partners agreeing to share responsibility for financial and domestic chores, but it was invariably the woman who was left with the latter—especially when the children came!

But that was all in the future—heck, she'd only met Peter two weeks ago!—and pushing aside all thought of him, she settled down to work.

In the event, she become so absorbed she had no time to go home to change before meeting her stepfather. But her red Valentino suit was suitable for day or evening, and slipping on a pair of thick gold earrings—part of the 'emergency kit' she kept in her desk drawer—she headed for the restaurant.

Robert was already seated when she arrived, and as she crossed the room every male eye followed her progress; not surprising though, for even in a city famed for its lovely women she was outstanding.

Five feet eight without shoes, she never made any concession to her height, always wearing the heels that fashion decreed, be they pumps or stilettos. Her colouring was typically Californian: streaked honey-blonde hair, and a peaches-and-cream complexion with a sprinkling of freckles brought out by the sun. Her slight irregularity of feature stopped her from being a chocolate-box beauty, but she was all the more arresting because of it. Her nose tip-tilted slightly, her mouth was generously wide with a full, softly curving lower lip, and her chin was square and determined. High cheekbones enhanced her wide-apart eyes, which glowed like sapphires when she was happy, and deepened to cobalt when she was not.

Yet she had little conceit about her appearance, accepting with gratitude that full breasts, tapering down to a small waist, allied to a swinging walk from nicely rounded hips, were attributes bound to attract attention.

'I enjoy seeing the men ogling you!' Robert smiled as he stood up to kiss her. 'They probably think you're my dolly bird, which does wonders for an old man's ego!'

'Old my foot!' snorted Leslie, though she had to admit her stepfather looked every one of his sixty-six years tonight. 'Half my boy-friends don't have your drive and energy.'

Looking pleased at the compliment, he drained his Martini. 'Have one?' he asked as he set down the glass and signalled the waiter.

'Mind if I make it a Bloody Mary?' she smiled. 'It kind of goes with my afternoon!'

'Like that, eh?'

'Like that.'

As their meal progressed, she purposely discussed her various problems, intent on taking his mind off his own. She did not refer to the divorce settlement, and by the evening's end the subject had still not been raised.

'If you aren't doing anything on Sunday,' Robert said outside the restaurant, 'perhaps we'll take the boat out.'

'Sounds great—if you don't mind me bringing my date along.'

'I'd be delighted. I'll call you at the weekend.'

By the time Leslie reached her apartment, south of Beverly Hills, she was more than ready for bed. It had been a long day, and a particularly unpleasant one; the sort it was best to forget.

Entering her living-room, she switched on the lamps. An interior designer, they said, reflected her style in her home, and this was also true of architects, for Leslie's apartment was a skilful combination of functional contemporary and Art Deco. Charles Eames chairs married well with an Aalvar Aalto tea-trolley that served as a bar, and a splendid lacquered Adnet cabinet housed her best china and cutlery; all set off by a white terrazzo-tiled floor and glossy white walls.

It was too stark a décor for her stepfather's taste, which veered to the traditional, as did many of her clients', with the result that she waged a constant battle with her conscience when designing homes for them. But until she could afford complete independence—she had refused any further financial help from Robert—she had to accept whatever commissions came her way.

The remainder of the week flew by, her evenings occupied as fully as her days, so that by the time Saturday dawned, hot and clear, she was ready for a day aboard her stepfather's boat. Despite several attempts to contact him and see what time she and Peter were expected next morning, she could not get a reply, and deciding the line was out of order, she drove to his home.

There was little traffic on the road and she soon drew up outside his split-level. His Mercedes was in the driveway and she was glad she hadn't made her journey in vain. She pressed the bell, and when there was no response she peered through one of the windows. A wall of glass in the living-room gave her a clear view of the terrace and pool, and she saw it was deserted. Puzzled, she walked to the back of the house. Occasionally the patio doors to the living-room were left unlocked, and she discovered this to be the case now.

'Robert?' she called, entering the house. 'Robert—it's me, Leslie. Where are you?'

All was silent, and she went in search of Kai, the houseman. His room and kitchen were empty, and surmising he had gone shopping and that her stepfather might have fallen asleep on his bed watching television, she went down the corridor to the main bedroom.

The door was shut but the television was on, and grinning, she knocked and entered, expecting to see Robert look up and greet her. But one glance at the twisted figure sprawled on the sheet, skin blanched, eyes staring, told her he had suffered a stroke!

Shock kept her momentarily rooted to the spot. Then with a sob she rushed to the telephone to call his doctor.

Only then did she notice the spilled bottle of sleeping pills on the floor near the bedside table, and the note with her name on it, on top of the clock radio. Shakily she read it, realising as she did that her stepfather had intended taking an overdose, but had been struck down before he could do so.

'My darling Leslie,' he had written, 'I'm addressing this letter to you rather than the boys, not because I love them less, but because you understand me better and appreciate how I feel. I have lost the business. Charlene sold her shares to Imtex this morning, without even giving me the chance to bid for them.

'I blame no one but myself for what's happened, and you mustn't either. Everyone told me what Charlene was, but I refused to listen, and I've paid the price.

'God bless and keep you, dear girl, and promise me you won't cry at my funeral. I've had a good life, and only regret the last four years.'

In the event, there had been no funeral, for Robert survived the stroke, though the prone figure in the flower-filled room in the nursing-home was nothing more than a living corpse.

It was impossible for Leslie not to blame Dane Jordan, regardless of how often she told herself Robert had contributed to his own misfortune. In court, the lawyer had made him appear a lecherous old man who had used his money to tempt an innocent girl into marriage, and then been so jealous and miserly that he had kept her a virtual prisoner.

How far from the truth this was! Robert's 'miserliness' had extended only to cancelling Charlene's credit cards after seeing the size of the bills she was running up, and it could hardly be considered 'jealousy' to lock her in her room when a drinking bout had rendered her incapable of driving her car—which she had been intent on doing.

Yet the lawyer's smooth tongue had depicted Robert as a monster, and there was no doubt in Leslie's mind that he was to blame for her stepfather's stroke as surely as if he had struck him down himself.

One day she might have the chance of making him pay for his callous behaviour, and if she did, she wouldn't hesitate to grasp it.

CHAPTER TWO

SEATED at her desk, Leslie glanced through her appointments. A Mr Jordan was due at half past two. Even today, six months after her stepfather's stroke, the name made her stomach tighten, though there were probably dozens, even hundreds of Jordans listed in the Los Angeles telephone directory.

Pushing her diary aside, she swivelled idly in her chair. Apart from the trauma of Robert's illness, these past months had been kind to her. She had won an award for a house she had designed in Coldwater Canyon, while another had featured in *Architectural Digest*—a prestigious glossy—which had pleased her senior partners sufficiently for them to give her a hefty raise.

Despite this—and no shortage of boy-friends—she wasn't happy. Bitterness and grief prevented her from living and thinking normally, for her weekly visits to Robert, who lived in a twilight world of his own, were a continual reminder of the man she held responsible for his living death.

Though she slept well at night through sheer exhaustion, many of her waking hours were disturbed by thinking up ways and means of destroying the lawyer's smug satisfaction with himself. But all her schemes were wild and impractical, and she discarded them as quickly as she thought of them. Would she always harbour a grudge against him, she wondered, or would time prove a healer?

Determinedly she went into her secretary's office—

14

Anne had called in sick this morning—to fetch the file on the client she was seeing after Mr Jordan.

'Where *is* everyone?' a male voice asked impatiently behind her.

Leslie swung round from the filing-cabinet, stifling a gasp as she recognised the tall, darkly handsome man glowering at her. It *was* Dane Jordan! She had envisaged such a meeting so often that, now he was actually facing her a she was speechless. Heart pounding, she went on staring at him, wondering if her fevered imagination had conjured him up. His next words showed it hadn't.

'Well, don't just stand there!' he barked. 'Take me to Mr Watson.'

Mr Watson indeed! Leslie nearly laughed in his face. What a shock he was in for! And several more if she could come up with them, she added darkly to herself.

'If you're Mr Jordan,' she said, 'your appointment isn't until two-thirty.'

'Two,' came the acid correction. 'It's *your* mistake, not mine. And don't expect me to pretend otherwise just because you're beautiful. Personally, I prefer efficiency in a secretary.'

'Really?' Leslie batted her eyes at him, giving him the full benefit of dazzling sapphire irises fringed by lashes so long and thick they were often mistaken for false. 'How do you feel about beautiful architects, Mr Jordan?'

His perfectly arched eyebrows rose in surprise. '*You're* the Watson I'm supposed to be seeing?'

'I am.'

'I'd just assumed you were a man. Sorry about that.'

Sorry you'll certainly be, she vowed, wondering how best to use this golden opportunity. She ached to give him a taste of the medicine he meted out to so many of his hapless victims, and now she had him in her sights, she simply had to think of something!

'I saw a house of yours in *Architectural Digest*,' he went on, 'and you showed an extremely interesting way of using space. So I'd like you to design a house for *me*.'

Resisting the urge to say she would far rather design a coffin for him, she led him into her office and waved him to sit down.

He did so, his wide shoulders blocking out the back of his tan leather chair. She was aware of him studying her, and was experienced enough to know he was impressed by what he saw.

Despite her dislike of him, she had to concede the admiration was mutual. He was six feet two at least, with the build of a rugger player. No, a coach might be a better analogy, taking into account the sprinkling of grey hair among the gleaming black at his temples. Piercing, deep-set eyes, almost as dark, were set beneath well-defined brows, while his nose was firm, the slight bump that marred it from perfection enhancing his rampant masculinity. His mouth was wide, his chin pugnacious, and his hands—which he used with such clever effect in court to punch home a point—were narrow, with tapering fingers.

She was thankful the desk separated them. To some degree at least, it lessened the pull of his personality.

'Do you have a site?' she asked crisply.

'Yes. In Bel Air. About two acres in all, and I want the existing house pulled down.'

Leslie didn't hide her surprise. 'Couldn't it be altered to suit you?'

He shook his head. 'If we compromise on the design, one or other of us will end up dissatisfied.'

'I can't see *you* compromising, Mr Jordan. But it seems a terrible waste to buy a house and demolish it.'

'I bought the land, Miss Watson. I consider the house expendable.'

People too, she thought bitterly, but aloud said: 'It's *your* money, of course, but I'd prefer not to waste it. Alterations are costly, but less so than starting from scratch.'

'Obstinate, aren't you?' he smiled. 'OK, how soon can you take a look at the place?'

'I'm tied up till the end of next week,' she lied. It would do him good to wait!

'Next week?' He looked affronted, then gave her another smile. 'What about one evening then, or the weekend maybe?'

'I work office hours, Mr Jordan.'

This was untrue, but she had no intention of obliging him. Besides, instinct told her that her lack of enthusiasm would make him all the keener to engage her.

'I'd be grateful if you *could* make it an evening,' he persisted, proving her theory. 'Then we can have dinner afterwards to discuss my needs.'

'As regards décor?' she queried icily.

'And food!' he grinned. 'After all, if you're designing my kitchen, you'll want to know whether I'm a vegetarian, a raw-food buff, or a meat-and-two-veg man.'

'I'd say crisp salad and rare steak,' she retorted. 'The bloodier the better!'

His silence was startled, then he burst out laughing. 'Was that an inspired guess or have you been checking up on me?'

'Neither. I simply know your professional reputation. You go for the jugular, Mr Jordan, so I assume you don't flinch at the sight of blood.'

His smile faded. 'I do my job—as I assume you do yours.'

She inclined her head, and flicked through her appointment book. 'Shall we say seven-thirty on Friday the seventh?'

'Morning or evening?'

'Morning.'

His eyes widened, and she noticed they were not as dark as she had originally thought, for there were gold flecks in them, sparked off by anger, she guessed happily, though he gave no sign of it as he answered her.

'Suits me fine.' He removed a card from the top pocket of his impeccably tailored grey silk jacket, and scribbled the address.

Leslie took it from him without bothering to look at it, not caring whether or not she gave an impression of lack of interest. She rose and held out her hand. 'Goodbye, Mr Jordan.'

His clasp was firm as he took it briefly in his. Then he strode across the room and out of the door, closing it carefully behind him.

Considering her lack of cordiality, she wouldn't have been surprised had he slammed it, and she saw his control as an added sign of his strength. He would make a formidable opponent, and she knew it wouldn't be easy to find his vulnerable spot. Still, nothing ventured nothing gained. The word 'gain' left a sour taste in her mouth, reminding her of her stepfather and all the other people who had fallen prey to Dane Jordan's ruthless inquisitions and greed-inspired demands.

When the day of their appointment finally came— the week had seemed so interminable that many times she had nearly called him to say she could see him earlier—she was no nearer a plan of action than when he had walked into her office, and hoped that meeting him again would provide her with the answer.

Familiarity with Bel Air made it easy for her to find the address he had given her. It was set high up in the lush green hills, and the skyline of Los Angeles acted as a stunning backdrop to the property, which was set some fifty feet back from the road, and hidden behind a high stone wall.

Dane Jordan was waiting for her in the driveway, standing beside an inexpensive Honda. Nastily she wondered if such a car was an affectation or a genuine desire to conserve fuel, as the sticker on the back proclaimed. If so, it was his only concession to economy, for his custom-tailored alpaca suit, pale blue silk shirt, and crocodile Gucci loafers shrieked money. His cuff-links, tie-pin, and Rolex quartz watch were all gold, and she wondered disparagingly if he wore a gold chain round his neck too!

'You're very punctual,' he greeted her. 'That gives you a distinct advantage over other women!'

'Clearly you've been mixing with the wrong kind,' she observed.

His smile thinned. 'Are you always this prickly, Miss Watson, or is there something about me that brings out the worst in you?'

First point to me! Leslie thought elatedly. A minor one, true, but it was useful to know he cared whether he was liked or not.

'I assure you I'm not treating you any differently from my other clients, Mr Jordan.'

'Then you must be a brilliant architect, for them to put up with you!'

'If you don't like my manners, you're free to find someone else.'

'I might just do that,' he drawled. 'But first I'll listen to your ideas, and see if your talent outweighs your temperament!' He dangled a door-key in front of her. 'Now, how about the grand tour?'

Leslie fell in step beside him. He towered above her, which was a sufficiently unusual occurrence for her to be aware of it; aware too of the muscles bulging beneath his navy jacket which, despite the precision of its cut, it did little to hide. It was as if he were deliberately proclaiming his masculinity. No wonder women chased after him to represent them in court and bed them out of it! He really was a handsome brute. Yet there was nothing brutish in his manner. If anything he was the epitome of the gentle giant.

'Could you give me some idea of what you want?' she asked as they entered the spacious entrance hall, with its central staircase leading up to a wide, circular landing.

For the next hour, as they tramped from room to room, he did just that, explaining that he required space for a private art gallery, a new master bedroom incorporating a jacuzzi and sauna, and an indoor squash court.

'I see no problems,' Leslie told him. 'If we knock down some of the interior walls, you'll have more than enough space.'

'Then I suggest you draw up the plans.'

'I can give you a pretty good idea here and now, if you have the imagination to picture it, Mr Jordan.'

He rubbed his cheek with a supple brown finger. 'I've been accused of many things, Miss Watson, but lack of imagination isn't one of them! Fire away.'

As concisely as possible, she did. It was interesting

that a man who hassled and interrupted to such good effect in court should be capable of listening in total silence, and only when she came to a final stop did he speak.

'You've grasped my requirements brilliantly, Miss Watson. If I had a hat, I'd take it off to you!'

She smiled faintly, reluctant to accept his praise. 'I'll let you have some drawings in a couple of weeks. Then you'll get a better idea of what I have in mind.'

'Can't you make it *one* week?'

'I'm afraid not. You'll have to take your place in the queue.'

'Seems I have no option,' he said. 'But I hope it only applies professionally. I'd like to take you to the Oscar Awards on Monday.'

Leslie was too astounded to reply, not so much because he had asked her out—she had been expecting it and had already decided to refuse—but that he should invite her to the Oscar Awards when tickets were harder to come by than moondust! Despite her earlier decision to turn him down, she was very tempted to accept, and as if aware of her hesitation, he gave a wry smile.

'I can see it's *me* you're undecided about, Miss Watson, not the ceremony! Am I really so unattractive that I have to resort to bribery?'

'Not at all. But I usually try to keep my business and social life separate. It's less complicated that way.'

'You say "usually". So I assume you sometimes make an exception?'

How typical of him to pounce on her slip of the tongue. 'You're very persistent, Mr Jordan,' she observed.

'Because you're very lovely, Miss Watson.'

'When we first met, you said you preferred

efficiency to beauty,' she reminded him.

'In business,' he chuckled, and she noticed how much younger he looked when he relaxed. Yet he still exuded an air of command, and she knew that whatever his mood, it would be dangerous to take him lightly.

'Perhaps now would be a good time for me to apologise for that remark,' he added ruefully.

'You mean it wasn't true?'

'I mean beauty plus intelligence is an unbeatable combination.' He watched her with darkening eyes. 'Am I forgiven?'

'As I'm accepting your invitation, I can't very well say no! What time shall I be ready?'

'I'll collect you at five.'

'So early?'

'They specifically ask you to be in your seats on time. Besides, it's fun watching the celebrities arrive.'

'You were lucky to get tickets,' she couldn't resist commenting as he walked her back to her car.

'It comes from having clients in high places!' he joked. 'I've handled half the divorce cases in Hollywood in the past few years, and as they say, one favour—and in some cases two or three!—deserves another.'

Leslie stiffened at this reminder of why she was agreeing to see him. What a shock he would get if she told him she was Robert Webb's stepdaughter, assuming he even remembered who Robert was! On the other hand, if he did, he probably thought of him as one more rich old man who had made a fool of himself over a girl young enough to be his daughter, and who deserved to pay handsomely for the short-lived pleasure.

'Don't you ever get a conscience about the kind of

law you practise?' she asked carefully.

He seemed surprised by the question. 'Why should I?'

'Because of the misery you cause. Wouldn't it be more rewarding to save marriages rather than kill them off?'

'I'm a lawyer, not a marriage-guidance counsellor.' One black eyebrow rose quizzically. 'Sounds like you've sat in on one of my cases!'

How far dared she go? she wondered. She didn't want to spoil a beautiful friendship before it had even begun! Yet she had to say something. 'I can't be impressed when a man has no respect for his own sex, Mr Jordan. And the way you try to destroy the husbands of your clients is appalling.'

His mouth tightened, and she knew she had overstepped the mark.

'I'm sorry,' she said. 'I've no right to be so critical.'

'You're entitled to your opinion. And your assessment of me isn't far short of the mark. I enjoy finding a man's Achilles' heel and pounding away at it until it's pierced. Maybe that's why I started off as a public prosecutor!'

And you clearly still see yourself as one, Leslie thought mutinously, but knew better than to say so. She had said enough for one day.

'Feel free to be honest with me too,' she said instead, as they reached her car. 'Like you, I respect the truth.'

'I'll remember that, though I don't promise to act on it. I don't want to risk having my face slapped!'

She had to laugh. 'Wise man! I pack a mean punch. But I'd still rather be told the truth. I work with four male architects, so I'm not used to being treated with kid gloves!'

'I'd like to treat you with chocolates and dolls,' he teased. 'When you laugh, you look like a child.'

'A twenty-six-year-old one,' she informed him. 'And in a city where twenty-two is considered ancient, I'm already over the hill!'

'Even at seventy-two you'll be a stunner,' he corrected. 'You've the kind of looks that last.' He examined her features with such slow deliberation that Leslie felt her cheeks grow warm. 'In fact I can't figure out why you haven't been snapped up—or are you divorced?'

'No,' she smiled. 'I'm still waiting for the right man to come along.'

'Not strictly a career girl, then?'

'Not strictly. I want a family and I'm prepared to take time off to have one.' She saw his features soften, and all at once got the first, faint glimmer of a plan that might, with luck, pay him back for the misery he had caused so many people. 'In fact,' she lied, 'I'd stay a housewife till my children were grown up.'

'You surprise me. Considering your earning power, that would be quite a sacrifice.'

'Money isn't everyone's Holy Grail, Mr Jordan.'

'Meaning it's mine?'

'Why else do you demand crippling alimony for women who clearly don't deserve it? Most of your clients only marry for what they can get out of it when they're divorced!'

'If a man's too stupid to realise the sort of wife he's chosen, he deserves to be taken to the cleaners,' he shrugged.

'Do *you* ever intend marrying?' she asked sweetly.

His lower lip curved up at the corners, as if he had been asked this many times before. 'No, I don't. I know better than to put my head in a noose! Anyway, why pay for what you can have for free?'

'Apart from which, wives grow old,' Leslie said gently.

'You have me taped, haven't you?'

I certainly have, she thought. And I'll soon have you bound, trussed and begging for mercy!

'You haven't answered me,' he said.

'I was just wondering whether you'll be dating twenty-year-olds when you're sixty!' she replied.

There was a telling silence.

'You've made your point, Miss Watson,' he murmured. 'But at least I'll avoid the ultimate stupidity of marrying them and being made a fool of by some lawyer like myself! I've worked too hard for what I have to give it away to some scheming gold-digger.'

'You've a pretty low opinion of women.'

'I've a pretty low opinion of people in general,' he replied candidly. 'I'm no great believer in the ultimate goodness of humanity.'

This was an area Leslie had no wish to explore; not that she disagreed with him on that score, but because she had no desire to find too many points of similarity with him! She had disliked him for too long to change her mind about him now.

Her glimmer of a plan was becoming a bright beam, and she saw how to put the first part of it into action. Although she had accepted his invitation to the Oscar Awards, she would let him down at the very last minute! That would make him furious as hell! Dane Jordan, normally seen at every smart function with a beautiful girl on his arm, would have to miss this one, or go alone!

'Why the smile?' he asked.

Instantly she composed her features. This man was too quick by half, and if she wasn't careful he would soon be reading *all* her thoughts.

'I was debating what to wear for the ceremony,' she murmured.

'You'd look good in anything,' he drawled. 'And better still in nothing.'

'Do you always say the expected?'

'Women *do* expect it!'

'This one would appreciate it if you didn't. Or does your mind only go along one groove?'

She heard the swift intake of his breath and knew he found her rudeness unusual and provoking.

'I'll try not to let it,' he said quietly. 'But you've got to admit you're not run-of-the-mill.'

'Now that's a compliment I appreciate, Mr Jordan,' she smiled.

'Do you think you could send me one back?'

'If you give me the opportunity!'

He laughed and opened the car door for her. 'I'll collect you at five sharp,' he repeated as she slipped into the driving-seat. 'Grab a sandwich first, though. The show goes on for hours, as you probably know.'

She nodded and turned on the ignition, driving away before he could say any more.

CHAPTER THREE

ALL weekend Leslie was in a fever of excitement, anticipating Dane Jordan's fury when she rang to cancel their date.

How late could she leave it? If he was collecting her at five he would have to be on his way by four-thirty. So she would call him at four twenty-five. Or would he perhaps change at his office? But no. She remembered his apartment was above it. Pity she didn't have a video phone to see his face when she told him she wouldn't be going with him! She hugged the thought to herself, enjoying it the nearer the time came.

Luckily Monday was busier than usual for her, and she spent most of it out of the office with a client, inspecting different building materials for the small apartment block she was designing for him.

It was three-thirty when they parted, and she went straight home. In the confines of her own four walls she paced nervously to and fro, looking at the telephone constantly but knowing she daren't pick it up until the last possible moment. The one thing she wasn't going to do was give Dane Jordan time to find a replacement for her!

At four-twenty precisely she opened the telephone directory and searched for the number of his apartment. To her dismay it wasn't listed! What a fool she was not have anticipated he would be ex-directory! With his reputation, some poor guy he had 'taken to the cleaners' might otherwise call and hurl abuse at him. But the minutes were ticking by and it

27

was imperative she contact him. With shaking fingers she dialled his office.

'Mr Jordan's left for the day,' the telephonist informed her, 'and we never give out his private number.'

'But I'm meant to be seeing him tonight,' Leslie said agitatedly, 'and I have to get in touch with him. I'm Leslie Watson, his architect.'

Almost at once she was put through to his secretary. It was now four-thirty and Leslie's nervousness mounted as she hurriedly reiterated that it was urgent she speak to him. What idiocy not to have thought of finding his number earlier. If this delay went on, he would be on his way to collect her before she could put him off.

'You may already have missed him,' his secretary echoed her thoughts, 'but I'll switch you through.'

Clutching the receiver tightly to her ear, Leslie listened to it ring, her dismay increasing as it remained unanswered. She was on the verge of replacing it when she heard his voice, incisive and impatient.

'Dane Jordan here.'

'It's Leslie Watson.' She made her voice tremulous. 'I'm sorry to have left it so late, but I—but I've the most appalling headache and I'm afraid I can't make it tonight.'

'You *what*?'

Leslie was thankful he couldn't see the grin splitting her face from ear to ear as she repeated her excuse. 'I know it's t-terribly short notice,' she stammered, 'but I k-kept hoping I'd feel better, instead of which I've been feeling progressively worse.'

'What have you taken for it?' he barked.

'I've special tablets, but they don't seem to have

worked. I'm just going to draw the blinds and go to bed. I'll be fine in the morning. I'm so sorry to let you down, Mr Jordan, do forgive me.'

Gently replacing the receiver, Leslie danced a little jig around the room.

'That's put paid to you, you egotistical swine!' she said out loud, and went into the kitchen to make herself a well-deserved coffee.

Standing by the window drinking it, she gazed down at the communal swimming-pool where some residents were sunbathing. Her life was too busy for her to make much use of it, for even at weekends she brought files home with her, or visited the various sites she was working on to see how things were progressing.

Robert had frequently chided her for being a workaholic, and she had tried to explain it away by saying it was because she wanted to be taken seriously as an architect.

'Even my tutors at college predicted I'd throw up my career to marry and have babies!' she had told him. 'And I'm determined to prove them wrong.'

'Even to the extent of *never* marrying and having babies?' Robert had teased.

'No, of course not. But I want to establish my name first.'

Remembering the conversation, she realised the years were passing fast. In a few months she would be twenty-seven, and if she wanted to be young enough to enjoy her children, she had better start thinking in terms of a husband. Trouble was, she hadn't met anyone she loved sufficiently to consider as a lifetime partner.

With a sigh she went to don a bikini. Then with sunglasses on her nose and book in hand, she went down to the pool and stretched out on a sunbed.

'Great to see you out here for a change.' It was Mrs Donovan, an elderly neighbour, sitting in the shade of a palm tree. 'It's about time you relaxed.'

Leslie smiled as she oiled her shapely limbs and lay back to let the warmth of the sun seep into her. She was crazy not to do this more often. Closing her eyes, she lay back luxuriously, feeling the tension ebb away from her, and acknowledging as it did how edgy she had been all weekend at the trick she had planned to play on Dane Jordan.

'Trying to make your headache worse?' A deeply sarcastic voice above her made her eyes fly open to stare into dark accusing ones.

In one swift glance she took in the towering figure in an impeccably cut white dinner-jacket that emphasised the jet-black hair, a lock of which had escaped as the man bent his head to glower at her.

'Of all the two-timing, conniving little . . .!' Words failed him, and he hauled her roughly to her feet, his hands hard as iron. 'I should have guessed you had something like this in mind when you accepted my invitation. You never had any intention of coming with me, did you?'

'I've got a headache,' she protested weakly.

'Like I'm pregnant!' He pulled her along the side of the pool to the back entrance of her block.

'Where are you taking me?' she gasped.

'To your apartment to change. You've barely ten minutes, so you'd better be quick!'

'I've no intention of changing.'

'Then I'll do it for you!'

They reached her front door, and grabbing the key from her canvas holdall, he inserted it in the lock.

'Get changed,' he repeated, pushing her into the hall. 'And no funny games either. I'm not in the mood.'

Nor did he look it. She had never seen anyone in such a monumental temper. Knowing when she was beaten, Leslie hurried to her bedroom and did as she was told, one part of her furious, the other admiring him for his perspicacity in guessing she had been lying. He really was a worthy opponent!

Despite herself she saw the humour of it, though it died quickly as she crossed to her dressing-table to brush her hair and saw the photograph of her mother and stepfather. Dane Jordan might have won this round, but she would make sure she won the next.

'You have five more minutes,' he called, rapping impatiently on the door, and she hurriedly zipped up her strapless red chiffon dress, stepped into high-heeled gold sandals and attached a pair of gold hoops to her lobes.

Lack of time forced her to keep her make-up to a minimum, but excitement had whipped colour into her cheeks and her eyes glowed like blue jewels. Not that the man waiting for her took any notice of her appearance, for the instant she came out of the bedroom he bundled her unceremoniously down to his car.

It was not a Honda this time, she noted, but a silver-grey Rolls, with a chauffeur in a uniform to match. Pity, she thought, sinking into the back, for it meant Dane Jordan could concentrate on *her*. Deliberately she turned her head to the mirror set into one of the side-panels, and fiddled with her hair, teasing out the long blonde strands into a more bouffant style.

'Leave your hair alone,' he said tersely. 'It's perfect as it is.'

'Why, thank you, Mr Jordan.'

'Dane, please. A man who came near to murdering you deserves to be called by his first name.'

Hiding a grin, Leslie settled back primly, her skirts wafting around her.

'Tell me,' he went on conversationally, 'what have I done to deserve your animus? I know you haven't liked me from the start, but I still can't figure out why.'

It was a great temptation to tell him, but it would give her only momentary pleasure, and she wanted a far more lasting satisfaction.

'Let's say your type doesn't appeal to me,' she shrugged. 'Conquests come too easily to you, and I don't intend being another one.'

'You haven't been asked yet!'

'But you will, won't you?'

'Probably,' he said drily. 'Though right now I'd rather wring your neck than take you to bed.'

The matter-of-fact manner in which he said this startled her, and she threw him an indignant look, which died as she saw the glitter of amusement lurking in his eyes. Damn him! He knew exactly how to rile her.

'You do yourself an injustice,' he went on more gently. 'I asked you out because I find you amusing as well as lovely to look at. Beautiful girls are a dime a dozen, and if that was all I wanted, I wouldn't aggravate myself pursuing *you*.'

'You're *pursuing* me?' she echoed.

'Why do you think I waited a week for you to come out and inspect my house?' he asked bluntly. 'People normally jump to it when I ask for something, and if they don't, I find someone who will.'

'Are you talking personally as well as professionally?'

'Both.'

'But you're willing to make an exception of me because of my mind?'

'That's right.' His eyes roamed over her slowly. 'You're beautiful, Leslie. One of the most beautiful girls I've seen, but you have something else that intrigues me even more.'

'My I.Q.'

'And your sharp tongue. The truth is, you don't bore me. And that makes you worth your weight in gold!'

Which I would be, if I married you, then engaged a lawyer like you to handle my divorce, she thought, quickly lowering her eyes so that he wouldn't see the glimmer in them glow into brilliant life. Instinctively she had hit on the perfect way of cutting him down to size. Talk about the biter being bit! She'd give Dane Jordan such a dose of his own medicine that he'd choke on it.

Vengeance was not an admirable trait, she knew, yet in this case she felt no pang of conscience. Indeed the more she thought of her idea, the more blissful was the prospect of dragging him through the courts and tabloids—as he had done to Robert and countless others. She would get a huge settlement out of him, then announce she was giving it all to charity!

'We're here.' He broke into her thoughts, and she dragged herself back to the present, fixing a smile on her face as she stepped from the car to confront the crowds come to ogle the celebrities.

As they wended their way into the auditorium, Dane was stopped frequently by people whose faces Leslie recognised from television and cinema screens, and it came forcibly home to her how well known he was. Even men from whom she knew he had extracted vast alimonies seemed to harbour no grudge as they slapped his shoulder and reminded him he hadn't come to dinner lately, or played the promised game of golf or tennis. Maybe if Robert had only had to give Charlene money, he too might have been equally sanguine about it. But because Charlene had been allowed to keep those damned shares ... With an effort Leslie pushed the whole ugly episode to the back of her mind and followed Dane to their seats.

The ceremony was exciting though long, and by the time it drew to a close, the headache she had pretended had become a real one. As they rose to leave, her vision misted over and she clutched on to the well-muscled arm next to her.

'I'm not acting now,' she said faintly. 'I-I honestly do have sledgehammers in my temples.'

'What have you eaten today?' he asked.

'A slice of toast and a cup of coffee.'

'You're a fool, do you know that?' he spoke tersely, though his hands were gentle as he guided her out to the street. 'Can you manage a hundred-yard walk? I arranged for Oaks to meet us a few blocks away, otherwise we'd be hours getting through the crush outside the theatre.'

She nodded meekly and he walked her slowly to the car. After an eternity she found herself sinking back against the soft leather, and she sighed with relief and closed her eyes, only opening them again when she felt a glass being put into her hand.

'Best cure for a headache,' Dane said. 'Drink it, then have this.'

'This' turned out to be a cracker and a slice of cheese.

'I always keep something in the car in case I forget to eat,' he explained, seeing her surprise.

'In the Honda too?' she asked with a faint smile, as

she downed the foamy concoction and nibbled at the snack.

'I keep food in all my cars,' he said drily, 'and a girl in every bedroom! I mean one has to be prepared, don't you think?'

A dimple came and went in her cheek. 'Definitely!'

Then remembering her brilliant plan, she knew that if she were successful there would be only one girl in one bedroom—herself!

And with a ring on her wedding finger too!

CHAPTER FOUR

LESLIE knew it would take all the wile and guile she possessed to get Dane to marry her, for he was a canny bachelor who had spent his adult life shying away from commitment to a female. Easier to net a swallow than this particular specimen of dominant masculinity!

In the depth of her heart she admitted that had she met him under different circumstances, she could easily have fallen in love with him, for he was handsome, intelligent, amusing ... The list was endless, and she hurriedly switched her thoughts back to her plan and what it entailed.

First, she would be the loving wife; make him so deliriously happy that he would boast of it to all his friends. Then, after lulling him into a state of bliss, she would start doing things to annoy him. With luck she might even goad him into losing his temper and hitting her! That should be good for another hundred thousand dollars at least, and make an even heftier sum for her to give to charity.

But first things first. Dane had categorically stated he would never marry, so how to disarm him? He was too clever to believe her if she professed to feel the same as he did, so she would take the wind out of his sails by saying the exact opposite! She would tell him marriage was her prime goal, and that she wouldn't consider anything else if and when she fell in love. Then she would inform him that as his ideas were diametrically opposed to hers, she would only agree to go on seeing him if they remained platonic friends.

'Platonic friends?' Dane echoed, his reaction bemused when she made this statement to him a few nights later at dinner.

'Why not? I'm sure there are plenty of occasions when you don't feel like making love and just want an intelligent girl to talk to.'

'I wouldn't say "plenty"!'

'You know what I mean.'

'Very clearly. But even if I agree to your suggestion, how do you know I still won't end up making a pass at you? After all, you're very passable material!'

'If you make one, I'll sidestep!'

He chuckled, then leaning back in his chair, eyed her speculatively. He had been out of town on a case and had called her the moment he had returned, sounding surprised when she had instantly agreed to have dinner with him. Now, of course, he knew why, and she could see his mind ticking over, as if looking for hidden snags.

'There's only one thing that puzzles me,' he said slowly. 'I can't believe there haven't been plenty of men willing to marry you.'

'Oh, there have. But I wasn't interested until I'd established my career.'

'But now you're ready to pick a husband?'

'When I find the right one, yes. Meanwhile it would be nice to know I can fall back on an interesting and good-looking escort.'

'While I can fall back on the female equivalent!'

'With the added advantage of knowing that as I've accepted you're not a marrying man, I won't be setting my sights on you.'

He quirked an eyebrow. 'There has to be a catch somewhere.'

'Not if we keep to the rules and only see one another when we've nothing better to do.'

'I can't think of anything better than being with you,' he admitted. 'If you didn't make marriage a stipulation, we could have a lot of fun.'

'If you keep harping on *that*, I won't see you at all.' Leslie gathered her purse and went to stand.

'Don't go,' he said swiftly, putting up a restraining hand. 'I'll play it your way, my angel, I promise.'

She nodded and gave him a sweet smile, convinced he was lying in his back teeth!

For two weeks Dane proved her wrong by keeping to their agreement, then all at once he started pursuing her with the ferocity of a hungry lion chasing a tasty doe, and only her daily calls to the nursing-home where her stepfather still lay in a coma prevented her from succumbing to his powerful charm.

But Dane was no fool, and realising his tactics were getting him nowhere, he reverted to his previous platonic behaviour, giving her no more than a chaste goodnight kiss on her cheek, and accepting her refusal to see him as often as he wanted.

Leslie knew he was playing a waiting game, and decided to give him a few more weeks' grace. If he didn't genuinely fall for her by then, she would have to call it a day.

She toyed with the notion of doing so now, for he was beginning to occupy too much of her thoughts for her peace of mind. On the evenings they didn't meet she kept wondering what he was doing and with whom, hating him for his ability to relegate her to one compartment of his life. Yet wasn't she doing the same with him, by dating other men? Unfortunately her dates no longer seemed pleasurable, and twice last week she had refused to see Peter Denver in the hope

Dane would call—which of course he hadn't.

Yet this week he had seen her three times, and she wondered if she was beginning to penetrate his armour. Well, she wouldn't know until she put it to the test.

They were dining at their favourite restaurant in Santa Monica when she decided to do so. Throughout their meal she kept giving heartfelt sighs, and though ravenous enough to eat a horse, merely picked at her food.

'Anything wrong?' Dane regarded her untouched plate.

'I'm afraid there is. You see, I—well, I don't think we should go on seeing each other. This must be the eighth time, and——'

'Twelfth,' he corrected. 'But who's counting, and why *shouldn't* we see each other?'

'Because I'm hardly dating anyone else—and that wasn't the idea. Elliot called me this evening, just after I'd agreed to see you, and I had to put him off, which didn't please him one bit.'

'So what?'

'So he wants to marry me. He's an architect and——'

'You could form your own partnership,' Dane said sarcastically, his tone giving Leslie a thrill of triumph.

'That was in my mind too,' she lied, 'except I don't love him.'

'Ah well, if you want love *and* marriage . . .'

'Don't tease,' she pouted. 'I'm very muddled and it's all your fault.'

'How come?'

'Because you've made me realise how boring Elliot is! So you see, you're bad for me.'

'And you're bad for me,' Dane acknowledged.

Leslie's heart sank. Was he going to take up her suggestion that they part? If he did, her entire scheme was in ruins.

'You're fun to be with,' he went on, 'and I find I'd rather be talking with you than making love to some dumb-bell.'

'I think that's extremely interesting, Dane. One day you might even change your mind about not getting married.'

'Pigs will fly first! Look, Leslie, I can't go on like this either. I want you so much it's driving me crazy!' He leaned across the table, and the pink glow of the sunset bordering the shimmering ocean beyond the window lent softness to his chiselled features. 'I'm putting my cards on the table because I don't want you accusing me of taking advantage of you. But this platonic idea of yours is giving me too many sleepless nights! Dammit, the thought of you is even interfering with my work, and that's never happened before! If you'd only come to bed with me, I'd be able to get you out of my system.'

Leslie's blood boiled with fury, but she managed to look ingenuous. 'How many times would it take? A week, a month?'

'I hadn't thought in terms of time,' he said thickly. 'All I know is I won't be able to think straight until I possess you.'

'I'd like that more than anything in the world,' she whispered, then drawing a deep breath, played her ace. 'I wasn't going to tell you how I feel about you, Dane, but hiding it seems so childish and—well, I want you to know how much I've grown to care for *you*.'

A broad beam transfigured his face.

'Then what are we waiting for?' he demanded

jubilantly. 'Love can be wonderful, sweetheart, and I'll show you.'

'How can you, when you've never *been* in love?'

'Well, I-I——'

'All you know is passion,' she went on in the same innocent voice, though she was hard put to it not to kick him on the shins. 'So, much as I long to say yes, I'm afraid I can't. It wouldn't work.'

'It will,' he persisted. 'Come away with me this weekend, and I'll prove it to you.'

'No.'

'But you just said you want me!'

'In marriage. You know how deeply I feel about keeping myself pure for my husband.'

As she spoke, Leslie realised the words came from her heart, and were not being said for effect. At last she knew exactly why she had always rejected casual affairs, why she had balked at the final surrender. Not that celibacy had been a problem, for she had sublimated her sexual energies in her work—until the past few months when she had found that work no longer satisfied her, and she had started envying her married friends who—predictably—envied *her*.

'Forget marriage for the moment,' pleaded Dane. 'Let me make love to you and show you how wonderful it can be.'

'If I said yes, I'd hate myself.'

He shook his head disbelievingly. 'I never thought I'd hear a sophisticated girl like you talk such rubbish! You know something, Leslie? You're too good to be true, and that's bad for me! So all things considered, I think we *should* call it a day.'

Shocked by his statement, she didn't know what to say.

'I can't see you changing,' he continued, 'and as I

won't, then I think your earlier suggestion was right. We should part while we're still friends. Besides, if you love me, as you say you do, you'll only get more hurt if we go on seeing each other. And the last thing I want is to have you on my conscience!'

What conscience? Leslie thought bitterly, but didn't waste her breath asking.

'If that's how you feel, Dane, there's no more to be said. Don't bother taking me home. I'll call a cab.'

'Don't be melodramatic. We have to go on meeting professionally. You're designing my house.'

'I'll ask one of the partners to take over.'

'Oh no, you won't! You're the one I'm paying and I've no intention of letting you walk out on the job.'

'You're a hard man,' she said bitterly, glad she could at least be truthful about something.

'So I've been told.'

But is he hard enough to stop seeing me? she questioned silently. At the moment he believed he could, yet she was banking on the hope that these past weeks—when she had fallen over herself to charm and disarm him—would be a powerful enough inducement to make him come back to her.

The long drive to Beverly Hills was a silent one, and as they drew up outside her apartment, Leslie thanked him sweetly for the evening.

'How can you be so calm?' he bit out, thumping his hand on the steering-wheel. 'I've told you I won't be taking you out again, yet you sit there looking at me as if—as if . . .'

'As if I still love you?' she finished sadly. 'But I do. Feelings don't die overnight.'

'But you should at least be angry with me.'

'How can I be, when I'm sorry for you? You're missing out on so much happiness, Dane.'

'Save your pity for those who need it,' he answered sourly. 'I prefer my freedom.'

'I know.'

She climbed out the car and walked away from him, but slowly, giving him the chance to come after her. It was only as she heard the screech of his tyres as he drove off that she realised he wouldn't, and chastened, she went across the lobby to the elevator.

Alone in her apartment, she was forced to acknowledge that Dane had acted admirably. At no stage had he pretended he loved her. He wanted her on his own terms, and having accepted that he couldn't get her, he had cut his losses. Perhaps it was best this way. Though she despised him for his courtroom tactics, she was by no means sure she was tough enough to be an avenging angel. She simply hoped that one day he would get his deserts, and that she would be around to see it.

That night she slept more soundly than she had in a long while, and awoke feeling refreshed and free.

She was standing by the window, sipping her first coffee of the day, when the telephone rang. Dane? Heart pounding, she forced herself to let it ring twice more before answering it. But it was a nurse from the clinic, quietly telling her that the man she had loved like a father had died of another stroke ten minutes ago.

'It was a merciful release for him,' the woman said sympathetically. 'Please remember that, and try not to be sad.'

Leslie reminded herself of this when Robert was laid to rest three days later. His two sons and their families had flown in for the funeral, and she was astounded to see Charlene there too, dramatic in black. What a nerve the girl had! But at least she had

the grace to sit at the back of the church, though she
could not resist coming over to Leslie at the graveside.

'I suppose you're surprised to see me here?'
Charlene asked in her soft Southern drawl.

'How perceptive of you!'

'You're easy to read,' the girl retorted. 'You've
never liked me, have you?'

'No. I always knew why you married Robert—and
you proved me right.'

'I only got what I was entitled to. Anyway, he was so
rich it didn't matter to him.'

'I wasn't thinking of the money,' Leslie said, 'but of
the way you sold your shares to Imtex. Robert would
have given you the same price if you'd offered them to
him.'

'I wanted to, but Dane wouldn't let me.'

Leslie stared at Charlene uncomprehendingly.

'That's shaken you, hasn't it?' the redhead drawled.
'Maybe if you'd known, you wouldn't have dated him.
Oh yes, I know you've been seeing him, because I saw
you together one night at Ma Maison. In fact I nearly
phoned to ask how you appeased your conscience! But
I can see from your face that Robert didn't tell you it
was Dane who did the deal with Imtex.'

'I don't believe you.'

'Ask Dane yourself. When they made me their offer
I wanted to ask Robert if he could match it, but Dane
said I'd be wasting my time because he wouldn't have
the ready cash, and I'd have to wait months for it.'

'You could have managed on your alimony,' Leslie
snapped.

'I know. But I had to do as Dane told me. When he
agreed to represent me, he also insisted on managing
my finances. Still, *you're* sharing in the money he's
earned from me, so there's no need to look so sour.

After all, he's using quite a whack of it to pay for the house you're building for him!'

Sickened, Leslie turned away. No need to ask why Charlene had come to the funeral! Not to see Robert laid to rest, that was for sure, but to destroy Leslie's association with Dane.

How furious she would be to know her disclosure had had the opposite effect, for Leslie's resolve not to seek personal revenge had disintegrated in the face of what she had just learned, and once again she determined to make Dane pay for his callous destruction of her stepfather's life.

CHAPTER FIVE

REALISING that getting Dane to marry her would be even harder than she had first thought, Leslie knew her only hope of wearing down his resistance was to play on his sympathy and pretend she couldn't live without him. On his own admission his interest in her went beyond the bedroom, and if she could get him to see how empty a purely sexual relationship was he might regard marriage to her as a real alternative.

The fact that they were still professionally associated made it easy for her to infiltrate into his life again, for rarely a day went by when he didn't go to his house to see how the work was progressing, and she always made sure she was there at the same time.

On the few occasions she missed him, she telephoned him with some trivial query, leaving him in no doubt that she was using it as an excuse to speak to him. And speak they did, often for half an hour or more, with Dane showing as much reluctance to say goodbye as she.

She soon sensed that meeting her or talking to her was becoming the focal point of his day, though he never suggested—nor even hinted—that they see each other socially. Damn him for taking her at her word! But he wasn't going to escape as easily as that, and she made a point of getting her dates to take her to all his favourite restaurants in the hope of bumping into him. When she did, which was at least fifty per cent of the time, he was always with a different girl—which meant he was still heartwhole!

Sometimes their tables were close, and Leslie feigned jealousy by watching him constantly in the hope that he would notice. She even went so far as to buy a couple of dresses a size too large for her, knowing it would make it seem as if she were losing weight, while a beautician friend taught her how to achieve a wan, hollow-eyed look.

Perusing the gossip columns, she became adept at picking out the parties Dane was likely to attend, and though they were the sort of glitzy affairs she had previously avoided like the plague, she knew enough 'right people' to secure invitations. A pretty girl was always a welcome addition, and admirers were soon clamouring for her attention, though she persisted in making it plain she had eyes only for Dane.

Yet if her lovesick act was having an effect on him, outwardly he gave no sign of it, but continued on his merry bachelor way, wining and dining a gaggle of brainless beauties, and behaving as if he adored every one of them. How could a man of intelligence waste his time on nitwits? Leslie constantly asked herself, though she knew the answer only too well! After all, what wolf would settle for one lamb when an entire flock was at his bidding!

The thought that she might be wasting her time trying to hook him occurred to her forcibly one morning when she met him at the house to discuss the new swimming-pool. He had clearly had a heavy night—though, irritatingly, the fine lines around his eyes and the hollows beneath them added interest to a face that was already too attractive for her peace of mind.

'Something wrong?' he asked, catching her gaze.

'No—why?'

'You have a funny expression on your face—as if

I've annoyed you.'

Leslie shrugged off his comment, reminding herself to watch her step. 'I was thinking you look tired.'

'I didn't get much sleep last night.'

'You should stop playing Casanova for a while, and curl up in bed with a book,' she told him.

'I tried that when I was dating *you*,' he said drily, 'and of the two, I'll take a girl!'

'Preferably a new one every time!' she added.

His hand rose and touched her silky hair. 'I'd happily settle for one, if it could be you.'

'Is that a proposal?'

'Not of marriage.' He dropped his hand abruptly, and she gave a heavy sigh.

'My luck I have to fall for a playboy misogynist!'

'That sounds like a contradiction in terms!'

'Not really. Lots of playboys basically fear women. That's why they avoid a relationship with one.' She turned a page of her notepad and stood poised, pen in hand. 'Now, shall we concentrate on the mosaics for the pool? Personally, I like blue and gold, but the choice is yours.'

If he was taken aback by her sudden change of subject, he gave no sign of it, though she was aware he wasn't concentrating on what she was saying, for his attention wandered and she had to repeat herself several times. Clearly she had given him food for thought, and if luck was with her, he might not find it too indigestible!

With the weekend looming, Leslie decided to kill two birds with one stone. Jack and Marybeth Foster, cousins on her mother's side, were staying at La Costa, a resort hotel near San Diego, where they had bought some land and asked her to build a holiday home for them. She had jumped at the chance, for she liked them immensely, and now that she had several suggestions in the drawing stage she decided to take them down and snatch a short vacation too. A change of scenery would do her good.

'Why not go for longer?' Jim McNaughton, one of the senior partners, suggested. 'You haven't had a holiday in a year, and it's beginning to tell.'

'You're a great morale-booster!' Leslie told him ruefully.

Warm brown eyes regarded her with fatherly concern. 'You're still the most beautiful architect in Los Angeles—but you look a tired one!'

'Enough said!' Leslie grinned, 'I'll take your advice and see you in a week.'

Next morning saw her bowling along the highway, delighting in the smogless blue sky and golden sunshine. For the first time in months she felt carefree and relaxed. The open windows and sunshine roof of her car created a refreshing cross-breeze that ruffled her hair, and she pulled it loose from its restricting pony-tail and tossed the ribbon on the back seat, next to her tennis racket and golf clubs. It was ages since she had played either, but she knew there would be no shortage of partners, La Costa boasting more than two dozen courts and a championship golf-course. The hotel was also a health spa, which was the main reason her cousins were there!

'Putting on weight is a helluva lot more fun than taking it off,' her cousin Jack grumbled that evening, as he watched Leslie tuck into a praline ice-cream topped by toasted nuts.

'You're not making me feel the least bit guilty!' Leslie rejoined, having decided that while on vacation she would eat to her heart's content and to hell with Dane Jordan.

'Glad to hear it,' grinned Jack. 'I'd hate to think I was cramping your appetite!'

'It was our European trip which did the final damage,' Marybeth, a plump and pretty forty-year-old, added. 'Three-star menus every day put on three pounds every night!'

Husband and wife exchanged glances and laughed, and Leslie basked in their happy companionship. So much for Dane and his sour views on marriage, when there were couples like Jack and Marybeth to give the lie to his cynicism! Jack had started work as a car salesman and now had one of the largest automobile franchises in San Francisco. He and Marybeth made no secret about enjoying the fruits of his success either, and were always fun to be with.

'Why wait till you're old before enjoying your money?' was his favourite dictum, and he had put it into practice by deciding to build a holiday home as close to La Costa as possible. 'That way I can diet here by day and sleep in my own bed at night!'

'We can look over the plans after dinner,' Leslie suggested now.

'You look too tired, honey,' said Marybeth. 'Leave it till tomorrow afternoon. We're having the flab massaged off in the morning.'

At three next day, Leslie went to their suite with her drawings. She had worked out various designs but personally liked only one of them. However, it was important to give a client a choice—even when they were relatives.

'You'll have to make do with me,' Jack apologised, opening the door at her knock. 'Marybeth got her appointment wrong, and is having a massage right now.'

'Shall we leave it till later, then?'

'No. If I don't work with *you*, I'll have to work out in the gym!'

Laughing, Leslie spread her drawings on the table, and for the rest of the afternoon they went through them in detail. To her delight, Jack chose her favourite design, said he didn't want to alter a thing, and suggested they open a bottle of champagne to celebrate.

'You're here to diet,' Leslie reminded him.

'What the heck! I feel like celebrating.'

Several glasses later, they were both in mellow mood as they reminisced about the past. Before Leslie's mother had married Robert, Jack had been like a protective brother to her, and to this day Leslie looked on him as an uncle.

'I'd better go and shower,' she said reluctantly, draining her glass. 'It's after five and I know you like to eat early.' Although there was a separate dining-room for health spa clients, the three of them dined each evening in the main restaurant.

'I hope Marybeth will approve of the plans,' she added as she went to the door.

'We're so much alike,' said Jack, 'she's bound to.'

'You're the only husband I know who never says his wife doesn't understand him!' Leslie laughed, stepping into the hall.

'Too right,' he agreed in his hearty salesman's voice, and glanced at the champagne in his hand. 'If she discovers I cheated on her this afternoon, all hell will break loose!'

'Tell her a redhead tempted you and you couldn't resist!'

A flash of white caught her eye, and half turning, she saw a broad-shouldered man in tennis gear striding towards her. For an instant she couldn't believe her eyes. Dane here? Was it pure chance or had he come in search of her?

'She knows me too well to fall for that one.' Jack was speaking again, and Leslie forced herself to listen. 'Anyway, I'm a man, not a mouse, and I can do as I please.' He flung an arm across his young cousin's shoulders. 'I never realised how talented you were until this afternoon. You're everything I every hoped you'd be.'

'Thanks.' She kissed his cheek. 'If I need a reference, I'll know where to come!'

'You can count on that, honey. See you later.'

As Jack closed the door of his suite, Leslie gave her attention to Dane. His short-sleeved Lacoste shirt revealed muscular arms, and the black hairs on his chest were visible through the fine white cotton. She was painfully aware of the brief shorts covering narrow hips above bronzed, sinewy legs, and wished he had chosen another resort instead of coming here and ruining her chance of forgetting him for a few days.

'Hello there!' She forced a smile to her face. 'What a surprise!'

'You can say that again!' He sounded and looked furious, his shoulders aggressively square, his mouth tight.

'What's that supposed to mean?' She favoured him with one of her most melting looks.

'Save the goo-goo eyes for the raunchy friend you've just left,' he snapped.

For an instant Leslie thought she had misheard him. Surely Dane didn't think . . .? But the glitter in the brown eyes that travelled over her confirmed that he most certainly did!

'Don't be silly,' she said aloud. 'Jack's a client, and a cousin.'

'And I'm an apple and a pear!' Dane said furiously.

'But it's true,' she insisted. What irony if she lost Dane through a genuine misunderstanding! It was something she couldn't let happen—not after the sleepless nights and hunger-filled days she had spent trying to snare him. 'Jack *is* my cousin, and I was in his suite discussing plans for a house I'm building for him and his wife. He's from San Francisco and——'

'Spare me the life history,' Dane cut in. 'I heard everything he said to you, including the bit about cheating on his wife, and how you were everything he'd ever hoped for! I always knew you'd be pretty hot stuff once you let yourself go, but like a fool I believed you when you said you were waiting till you married!' Angrily he grabbed her shoulders. 'If I'd known you were two-timing me, you'd have have been in my bed so fast it would have made your head spin!'

'I wasn't two-timing you,' Leslie protested, trying unsuccessfully to pull free of him. 'I've never cheated on you with any man.'

'Doesn't this so-called "cousin" count?' came the sarcastic question. 'Or is it a woman in drag?'

'Don't be stupid!' Anger gave Leslie the strength to wrench free of Dane's hold, and also to forget her sweetness-and-light act. 'I don't need to defend *my* morals to someone who doesn't even know the meaning of the word!'

Not waiting to hear his reply, she ran along the corridor to the elevator. The door opened immediately, and with a sigh of relief she stepped inside.

Back in her room, Leslie had plenty to think about as she showered and changed. Why was Dane at La Costa? Was it coincidence or had he come to look for her with reconciliation in mind?

One thing was sure. He was livid over Jack, which either meant wounded pride or jealousy. The idea of his being jealous was such a cheering thought that it lifted her mood, and she was bubbling with plans for Dane's future misery when she joined her cousins in the bar. Yet outwardly she was a tall, cool blonde in almond-pink silk, her simple camisole top and matching trousers making the other women look overdressed.

'Had a good massage?' Leslie asked Marybeth, taking a seat opposite her.

'Fantastic. And so are the plans for the house. Jack showed them to me.'

Her husband stopped a waiter. 'What'll you have, Leslie?'

'A Bloody Mary.'

'How about a vodka and caviar?'

'Oh sure,' she laughed, her silky hair abounce as she flung back her head. 'With a little *foie gras* on the side, to help it go down!'

'Why not, if it's what you fancy?'

'I also fancy a mink coat slung over the front seat of a Ferrari!' she teased.

'I'll get it for you,' he grinned, 'and knock it off your fee!'

'Do that, and I'll build you a house with no windows!'

Her cousins laughed, Marybeth stopping as she saw Leslie's eyes stray to the bar entrance.

'Are you expecting someone, honey?'

Why deny it? Leslie thought, especially since she and Dane were sure to bump into each other again. In fact it was essential they did.

'Not exactly,' she murmured. 'But . . . well . . .' She

glanced at Jack. 'After I left your suite this afternoon, I bumped into a client of mine—who's also an ex-boyfriend.'

Briefly she recounted what Dane had thought, and Jack, after a look of comical amazement, roared with laughter.

'I'm glad he thinks I could pull a young beauty like you!'

'It may be good for *your* ego,' his wife chided, 'but not for Leslie's!' Marybeth gave her a keen glance. 'Still, if he's an ex of yours, it's none of his business what you do!'

'Unless he still cares for you,' said Jack.

'And unless you care for *him*,' Marybeth added.

It was on the tip of Leslie's tongue to tell them who Dane was and why she had set her sights on marrying him, but she was reluctant to involve anyone else in her deception. She would have to say *something*, though.

'I care for him very much,' she murmured, 'and I think he feels the same about me. Trouble is, he's dead set against marriage, so I stopped seeing him.' At least *that* was no lie.

'So that's why he blew his top when he thought he'd caught you with Jack?' chortled Marybeth.

'Yes. And I'm hoping it's more than pique. That's why I want to meet him and clear the air.'

'Why not ask him to join us for dinner?' Jack suggested. 'Then he'll see for himself that we——'

He stopped as Leslie touched his arm and flicked her eyes towards the man entering the bar.

Six foot two of brawn and brain stood in the doorway, looking around him. A navy and white check jacket made his tan appear darker, his hair blue-black. The contrast with her own colouring could not have been more marked. Night and day, she mused, and realised it depicted their characters too. She went on watching him, tensing as he suddenly spied her and, without hesitation, headed in her direction.

'Dane, I take it?' Marybeth muttered.

'None other,' said Leslie.

'What a dish! I know what *I'd* have done if he'd asked me to choose between an affair and nothing!'

Leslie wondered if she would have done the same as Marybeth had the circumstances been different. Before she could reach a conclusion, Dane was standing beside her.

'Seems I owe you an apology,' he said gruffly.

'What for?' she questioned, determined not to let this worm off the hook. Let him wriggle!

'Not only for my stupid accusation,' he said, 'but my bigger stupidity in not accepting your word that I was wrong. After I cooled down, I knew you weren't the type to lie about your feelings.'

His reasoning—bearing in mind his cynicism—was complimentary, and Leslie gave him a slightly warmer smile and introduced him to her cousins.

'Sorry to barge in on you like this,' Dane apologised. 'I called Leslie's room, but she'd already left.'

'No sweat,' shrugged Jack. 'Sit down and have a drink.'

Accepting the offer, Dane took the chair next to Marybeth.

'So you're the famous divorce lawyer?' she said, recognising the name though luckily not associating it with Robert's divorce, for she and Jack had been abroad at the time.

'I'm afraid so,' he replied.

'Afraid, Mr Jordan?' This from Jack. 'But your

reputation's legend.'

'Which is my problem. Wives get ideas just by looking at me!'

'I can see why,' Marybeth intoned, and Dane chuckled.

'But I wasn't talking about that kind of idea, Mrs Foster!'

'There's no likelihood of any other at *this* table,' her husband put in. 'Everything's in *her* name already!' He called the waiter and Dane asked for Scotch on the rocks.

'Staying long?' asked Marybeth with a look of innocence.

'For the weekend.'

'Are you on your own?'

Leslie held her breath, and out of the corner of her eye saw an amused quirk lift Dane's mouth, making it obvious he wasn't taken in by Marybeth's nonchalance.

'I'm visiting a friend of mine,' he said. 'He's here to lose weight.'

Leslie breathed easier. At least she wouldn't have to play second fiddle to one of his dumb-bells!

'How about you and your friend joining us for dinner?' Jack ventured.

'He's got a date,' Dane replied, 'and I'm hoping I can say the same.' He raised an eyebrow in Leslie's direction. 'I'd like to take this young woman to dinner—if you don't mind losing her for an evening.'

Good old Dane! Leslie thought wryly, taking her for granted again. But then why shouldn't he, when she had made herself act like a doormat these past few months in her efforts to win him over.

'Mind?' Marybeth squeaked. 'Why, we're delighted to be rid of her! Watching her stuff herself while we nibble at rabbit's food is enough to make a saint envious!'

Laughing, Dane glanced at the Patek Philippe watch on his wrist. Like everything else he wore, it was the best money could buy. 'I think we'd best get going. I've a reservation at The Chart Room and I don't want to lose it.'

'When did you book?' Leslie asked curiously as she followed him to the car park.

'Earlier this evening. And before you accuse me of taking you for granted, I assure you from past experience that it's the last thing I'd do! The Chart Room's the most popular restaurant in La Jolla'—he named the neighbouring town—'and I didn't want to lose out on a reservation if you agreed to come with me.'

A likely story! Even if she had turned him down, he would have had no problem finding an attractive companion, and he was conceited enough to know it!

They reached his car and she settled into her seat. The silk of her trousers clung to her shapely legs, and she was aware of his admiring gaze on them.

'Is this your first time in La Costa?' she asked quickly.

'No. I've been here several times.' He paused. 'Always alone.'

'Really?' She pretended unconcern.

'Scout's honour. Even I need a rest between beds!'

'Glad to hear it. At least I won't have to defend my honour tonight.'

'Don't bank on it,' he flipped back. 'My batteries are completely recharged!'

'In which case I'd better put a spanner in the works,' she said as he switched on the engine. 'No punctures in the middle of nowhere, and no pretending you've run out of gas!'

'Give me credit for a bit more subtlety!' he reproached her. 'I was thinking of using "My God, I'm dying, I need the kiss of life"!'

It was impossible to keep a straight face, and her laughter rang out. 'That's certainly original!'

'I always try to be.'

Deciding it was safer to ignore this, she watched the passing scenery. There was little traffic on the road to La Jolla, and the Mercedes ate up the miles. She hadn't driven in this car before, and asked him if it was new.

'Rented,' he replied. 'I flew down.'

'I can give you a lift back, if you stay a few days longer.'

'I'd like nothing better, but I have to be in court first thing Monday, so I'm leaving tomorrow.'

'Another juicy divorce case?' Leslie tried unsuccessfully to keep the contempt from her voice.

'Yes.' He chose to ignore her criticism. 'A husband of seventy walked out on his wife and married a twenty-one-year-old—who's now divorcing *him*!'

'How many millions are you trying to get for *her*?' Leslie asked sarcastically.

Dane's mouth tightened. 'Don't expect me to go easy on a man who walked out on gold to marry dross.'

'They say love is blind,' she persisted.

'They also say there's none so blind as those who don't *want* to see,' he retaliated.

Leslie sighed, knowing he was right. 'Handling all those sordid cases has made you a cynic,' she told him.

'I was cynical long before I became a lawyer.'

She longed to know why. An unhappy love affair in his youth would hardly have marked him for life.

'It hasn't anything to do with some youthful peccadillo either,' he added, divining her thoughts.

She waited for him to say what it did have to do with, but his silence told her she was waiting in vain. But then he never discussed his past. On the rare occasions she had led the conversation that way, he had adroitly changed the subject.

A short while later he swung into the car park of the pink-washed Spanish-style restaurant, and turning swiftly gave her a quick kiss on the mouth before getting out to open the door for her.

'Let's go,' he pronounced, clasping her hand in his.

But where will we be going tomorrow and all the other tomorrows? Leslie wondered as she stepped from the car, and knew it was a question that would soon have to be answered.

CHAPTER SIX

ENTERING the softly lit room, with piped music soothing the ear rather than assualting it, Leslie and Dane were led to one of the tables encircling a small dance-floor.

As always when she was with him, she was not only aware of being with the best-looking man in the room, but with one whose confidence made him his own man, answerable to no one. Yet no human being should consider themselves an island, and Dane's lack of compassion for his fellow men minimised him greatly.

'I detect some dark thoughts going on in that lovely head of yours,' he chided. 'I hope they're not about me.'

'I do occasionally think of other things,' she said demurely.

'Such as?'

'The state of the economy, nuclear war, human rights. Unimportant issues compared with my feelings for you—but then we're all entitled to a little light relief!'

'You've an answer for everything, even if it's not always truthful! No wonder I find you intriguing.'

'But not as intriguing as your ever-changing nymphs,' she declared. 'I'm beginning to realise why I've failed to capture you, Dane. I'm too old for you!'

'You know damn well that the problem is your crazy insistence on marriage,' he grunted.

'You make marriage sound like a sin!'

'It is to *me*.'

As she opened her mouth to make a snappy retort, he put up a hand to silence her.

'No, Leslie. Let's call it quits and declare a truce.'

'It seems the only solution,' she sighed, and picking up the menu, studied it. 'I don't know about you, but I'm ravenous.'

'Glad to hear it.' His appraisal of her held more than a hint of speculation. 'These past few weeks, whenever I saw you in a restaurant, I couldn't help noticing you only pecked at your food.'

Leslie kept her lids lowered. From the moment Marybeth had unwittingly given her away in the bar by saying how heartily she ate, she had been waiting for Dane to make this comment.

'I did lose my appetite for a while,' she lied. 'The mere sight of food made me feel quite ill. But my doctor prescribed some fantastic new pills.' She ran her tongue along her lips, giving an award-winning act of hesitancy. 'I—er—I just worry in case I have to take them too long. They have some pretty rotten side-effects!'

'Such as?'

'Hair-loss,' she fingered a silky blonde tress, 'and blurred vision. Still, anything's better than anorexia!'

Dane swallowed the remainder of his Scotch, his serious expression denoting that he had swallowed her lie along with it. With difficulty she kept a straight face.

'Don't blame yourself because I can't get over you,' she pressed on, gently rubbing salt in the wound. 'It's not your fault you don't love me.'

She waited hopefully for him to deny it, but all she got was another assessing look as he raked his hands through his hair, ruffling the dark strands. The unruliness accentuated the grey flecks, and made him look more vulnerable. Yet when he spoke, he showed total command of the situation.

'I think it would be more sensible if you got someone else in your firm to take over the completion of my house. Then you won't have any need to see me.'

Hiding her fury at this suggestion—and she, poor fool, had actually believed he was weakening!—Leslie forced a slight catch to her voice.

'It makes no difference whether I see you or not. I still keep thinking of you. But that's my problem, Dane, and sooner or later I'll work it out. You know what they say about tunnels? No matter how long and dark they seem, there's always a light at the end of them. So stop worrying about me.'

'I can't help it. Are you sure you want to go on handling the house?'

'I'm positive.'

Although he allowed her the final word, Dane was unusually subdued as their meal progressed, and she was delighted to think he had food for thought as well as food to digest.

'That was the best duck *à l'orange* I've had in years,' she pronounced as the waiter removed their plates.

'I'm glad you enjoyed it,' said Dane. 'Care for dessert?'

She shook her head, and he signalled for coffee, then glanced towards the dance-floor.

Nodding, Leslie rose and preceded him on to it. It was not the first time they had danced together, and as always their bodies moved in unison, their steps effortless. They didn't speak and she rested her cheek against his shoulder, making a soft, murmuring sound as she did. The tempo slowed, and he pressed her closer to him and nuzzled his face in her hair.

'Delicious,' he murmured. 'Delicate as Arpège, with a slight hint of Shalimar—or is it Mitsouko?'

'Neither. It's Femme.'

'Hmm. I must remember it.'

So that he could dole it out to one of his dolly-birds, Leslie thought waspishly, and wished she had kept the name to herself. Yet it was difficult to think sour thoughts when his closeness was having such a sweet and unwelcome effect on her. She was too aware of the hardness of his chest against her breasts, the firmness of his stomach, the steel-like muscles of his thighs pressing against hers. He was barely dancing; it was more a languid, swaying motion to the music, like making love standing up.

Her instinct was to pull away, but she quickly reminded herself she was meant to be in love with him and should show some response. The trouble was, it didn't require much effort, for his nearness was arousing her in the most unnerving way, making her question her long-held belief that sex without love was meaningless.

His fingers caressed the soft skin at the nape of her neck, then trailed across her back to her spine, his touch light as a butterfly's wing. She tried to fix her mind on other things: the people around her, the décor, the view of the shimmering ocean through the wide windows. But nothing helped. Slowly, insistently, her senses took possession of her brain, until she was lost in the warmth of him, the smell of him, the feel of him.

'I think our coffee's getting cold,' she managed to croak out, looking across at their table.

'I'm happy to let it ice up for the pleasure of holding you a bit longer!'

'And have me die of thirst?'

'You're having *me* die of hunger—for you!'

'Poor Dane,' she teased.

'Hard-hearted Leslie,' he rejoined, and led her back to the table.

As he went to refill her wine-glass, she stopped him. She had drunk more than half a bottle of Pinot Noir, and wouldn't answer for herself if she had any more. But maybe that was what he was hoping for!

'Just black coffee,' she stated. 'Extra strong.'

Dane half-smiled, as though divining her thoughts. 'Working on anything interesting?' he asked, finishing off the wine.

'As a matter of fact I am. A new church in Palo Alto.' She named the city that was the home of Stanford University.

'My old stomping ground,' he smiled. 'I got my degree there.'

'Somehow I imagined you at Harvard.'

'You imagine me in many places,' he quipped, and Leslie instantly had a vision of dozens of beds filled with blondes, redheads and brunettes.

Pushing the fantasy aside, she realised how little she knew of Dane's background. She had been careful about questioning him in case he did the same with her and she gave herself away. But having gained in confidence, she felt she could handle anything he threw at her.

'Are you from California?' she asked.

'From across the border—Portland.'

'Nice city. I was there for a week last year discussing plans for a school—but it didn't come to anything.'

'You must have been disappointed.'

'I was. Don't *you* feel let down when you lose a case?'

'I've never lost one. I've been lucky, I guess.'

'False modesty doesn't become you, Dane! Much as I loathe what you do, I have to admit you're top of your field.'

'You've a marvellous knack of turning a compliment into an insult! Considering how you feel about my profession, I'm surprised you want to marry me.'

'So am I!' Leslie had been ready for this remark for months, and fielded it expertly. 'But one can't fall in love—or out of it—to order. You're the last person in the world I wanted to love, yet I couldn't prevent it happening, and now I'm willing to take you warts and all.'

'Your way with words continues to underwhelm me!' grunted Dane. 'Are you always so damn blunt?'

'Would you rather I put on an act, like your other girl-friends?'

'Don't you dare! As I've already said, your honesty is one of the things I like about you.' Dark eyes glinted with humour. 'Though I won't deny that an occasional white lie wouldn't hurt your cause!'

'You're so clever you'd see through them.'

'I guess I would, at that. So I'll have to take *you* warts and all!'

Unexpectedly, Leslie's conscience prickled. Until Dane had come into her life, she had considered herself perfectly straightforward. Yet now she was as straight as a corkscrew!

'Where do we go from here?' Dane asked suddenly. 'You've got to admit we both have the same end in mind.'

'But mine leads to it via the altar, and yours is strictly up the garden path!'

Against his will, he laughed. 'You're such a delight

to be with, Leslie. If only you weren't so old-fashioned!'

'If I were different, you might feel differently about me too.'

'Take a chance and find out,' he invited.

'No.'

'You're so obstinate.'

'You're no Mr Malleable yourself!' Leslie retorted.

'Agreed. But at least I'm leading a full and happy life—unlike you. Dammit, Leslie, don't you ever feel sexually frustrated?'

'Quite often. But then I remember what marriage means to me, and I'm willing to wait.'

'Me too,' he said irritably. 'For ever!'

She gave a deep sigh. 'Don't you want children?'

'Eventually. But marriage is no longer a requisite, surely?'

'Depends where you live. America is more than California and New York, you know, and the young have enough problems growing up in the world, without the added burden of illegitimacy.'

Dane stared into his cup, pondering her remark. 'Could be you're right,' he conceded finally. 'But I still contend that marriage will eventually be viewed as an anachronism.'

'Which will make your particular talents—as a lawyer redundant!' she added mischievously. 'You'd better start saving for your retirement!'

'I can afford to retire now. I only work because I enjoy handling divorce.'

Leslie knew he was deliberately riling her, and refusing to rise to the bait, she changed the subject.

'Do you have parents?' she asked.

'Naturally! Contrary to your belief, I wasn't created in Frankenstein's laboratory!'

'You know what I mean,' she pouted. 'Are they still alive?'

'My mother is.'

'When did you lose your father?'

'In my early teens.'

There was a noticeable thinning of his mouth and she waited for him to continue, but he took another sip of coffee and remained silent.

'Any brothers and sisters?' she ventured.

Three sisters, all older than I am, and married, with families large enough to keep an adoring grandmother fully occupied.'

'So you're the only son?'

'And spoiled rotten—so don't bother saying it! But I was too independent to be a victim of smother-love!'

In spite of all he was saying, Leslie was still convinced his reluctance to form a binding relationship stemmed from something in his past. But what? It sounded secure enough, and he spoke fondly of his mother and sisters.

'Now I've told you about *my* family,' Dane put in, 'how about filling me in on yours?'

Leslie was glad she had rehearsed her answer, and she launched into it confidently. 'My parents are dead, and I was an only child. Most of my relatives live back East, but I can't stand cold weather and moved to California when I left college. That about sums it up.'

'Not really. I'd like to see more of the light and shade. A bright girl like you must have an interesting family tree.'

'Mind if I tell you another time?' Leslie made herself yawn prettily. 'I'm awfully tired.'

On the journey back to La Costa, she kept her eyes closed to discourage Dane from further questions. Not that she wasn't prepared for them, but tonight had been a strain from start to finish, and she was exhausted from being constantly on her mettle, feigning emotions she didn't feel. Only in the safety of her room could she relax and be herself again—and how she longed for it!

The touch of Dane's lips on hers—light and cool—made her eyes fly open. Instinctively she turned her head away, and surprisingly he didn't stop her.

'We've reached your castle, Sleeping Beauty.' Gently he drew her out of the car.

'It was a lovely evening,' she told him as they entered the hotel lobby.

'It's not over till we reach your bedroom door.'

'As long as you realise that's where it *is* over!'

'Scared you mightn't be able to resist me if I come in for a nightcap?'

His question was too close to home for comfort. 'How about a game of tennis tomorrow?' she parried. 'We could play mixed doubles if your friend can find himself a partner.'

'I'll ask him and let you know at breakfast. Meet me in the dining-room at nine. Or is that too early for you?'

'You've got to be kidding. I'm not a lying-in girl.'

'Because you've no one to lie in with! Do it with the right person, and I guarantee you'll find it more fun than getting up!'

'I'll take your word for it.'

'Try it for yourself—with me.'

Leslie sighed. 'You deserve an A-plus for persistence.'

'For performance too!' came the swift retort. 'Try me.'

'I will—on our wedding night!'

Dane chuckled. '*You* deserve an A-plus for *in*sistence!'

They had reached her bedroom, and as she took the key from her purse, he plucked it from her and opened the door. She crossed the threshold, hand extended for her key, but he shook his head.

'Not until I've kissed you goodnight.'

'You did that in the car,' she reminded him.

'That was a wake-up kiss. There's a world of difference.' He came closer and tilted her face up to his. 'I'll show you.'

His mouth came down on hers, warm and demanding, as were his hands, moving across her back and tracing the curves of her body, pressing them close to his. He made no attempt to hide his arousal, his clothes a scant barrier to his hardness.

Leslie tried to push him away, but he caught her wrists and edged her further into the room, closing the door with his foot.

Once again he took possession of her lips, running his tongue gently across them, then parting them to enter and explore the moist depths. She tried to break free, but it was hopeless. His hold was like a vice and his lips were already nuzzling the soft hollow of her throat, then moving along the smooth skin of her shoulders to the curve of her breasts, their nipples clearly visible beneath their thin covering.

'You know you want me,' he said thickly. 'Why fight it?'

Why indeed? she wondered, for his question had given her an idea. It was one born of desperation, for tonight had shown her how determined Dane was to stay single. But what would happen if she let him make love to her—not all the way, of course, but enough to give him a sample of the pleasures that could be his? It was a ploy as old as the hills, and one he might easily see through, but it was worth her taking the chance.

The main danger lay in her susceptibility to him, and being able to stop herself before the act of consummation. Yet she refused to think of the consequences of failure. She was gambling for high stakes, and it made the risk worthwhile.

'I'm not fighting you, Dane, only myself,' she whispered shakily. 'You know how much you mean to me and I . . .' She forced a note of panic into her voice. 'Please go. Don't make me do something I'll regret.'

'You won't regret it, sweetheart,' he said throatily, the quickening of his breathing giving her an indication of his excitement. 'You were made for love, and I'm going to show you how wonderful it can be.' Eyes darkened by desire ranged over her with such naked passion that she felt as if he were stripping her.

'No, Dane, I can't!'

'You can, darling.' Tenderly he kissed the palms of her hands, then flicked his tongue along the tips of her fingers. 'Don't be scared of me. I'll stop any time you want.'

Leslie had difficulty hiding a smile. That line had probably originated with Adam, and if Dane believed she would fall for it, he must think her as innocent as Eve. Well, he would soon discover that *her* bed wasn't going to be his Garden of Eden—more like Paradise Lost!

'You're the most wonderful man I've met,' she said huskily. 'You can be so thoughtful, so kind and gentle.'

She wondered if she were laying it on too thick, but his expression told her he was lapping it up like a puppy milk, and she marvelled at his kingsized ego. What pleasure she would get from deflating it!

'Take me to bed,' she moaned, leaning against him and running her fingers through his hair. 'Make love to me, Dane. I want you so much.'

'And I want you.' His voice throbbed with passion as he drew her down upon the bed.

Deftly he undid the tiny buttons of her bodice, and easing her free of it, cupped his lean, bronzed hands around her full breasts. Expertly his mouth claimed each rosebud nipple in turn, his tongue and teeth teasing one rosy peak and then the other, till she lay shuddering against him, wondering where she would find the strength to resist him.

His lips returned to hers, and she met him kiss for kiss, lost in an exhilarating joy that was swiftly spiralling out of control as he explored the most intimate parts of her body; touching, stroking, licking, caressing. Never had she believed she could respond with such fervour, and the sheer physical pleasure of his naked flesh upon her aroused her to such wanton desire to have his hardness inside her that her legs parted involuntarily, bidding him into the burning core of her; to take control, to assuage the gnawing ache.

'Now you're going to learn what love's all about!' Dane muttered fiercely, his mouth tracing a red-hot line of fire along hers.

If he hadn't spoken, Leslie would mindlessly have given him total possession of her. But the word 'love' was like a thunderclap in her ears, bringing her back to reality as nothing else could have done.

How dare he use the word love? It played no part in what they were doing; their bodies were merely responding to a biological urge.

Pushing him violently away, she rolled from

beneath him, gathering the sheet about her nakedness as she did.

'What the hell!' Dane flicked on the bedside light and peered at her. 'Is this some kind of game?'

'No. I'm just exercising my prerogative. You said if I didn't want to go all the way . . .'

Her voice was low as she put the distance of the room between them, and came to rest by the window. She felt safer here, less vulnerable to his very considerable physical presence. Nude, he was like a Greek god, his body a perfect combination of well-honed muscle and bone.

'You said you'd stop any time I wanted,' she reminded him, annoyed to find her voice shaking. 'Don't be angry with me, Dane.'

His mouth opened and shut again. She had him, and he knew it.

'Sex without marriage goes against everything I believe in,' she went on, hiding her triumph. 'But because I love you so much I thought I could go against that belief. But I find I can't and . . . Oh, Dane, I'm so sorry. Truly I am.'

'Sorry!' he echoed contemptuously. 'I'm the one who should be sorry! Sorry I made the mistake of thinking you were a flesh-and-blood woman.'

His voice lashed against her like a whip, and she was astonished he had so much control when only minutes ago he had been racked by passion.

'You won't make a fool of me again, Leslie.' Standing up, he gathered his scattered clothes from the floor and began to dress.

Silently she watched him. What more was there to say anyway? He was like a stranger, his mouth a narrow slit, a vein pulsing angrily at his temple. Poor Dane. How frustrated he was, and how thoroughly he disliked her! In an odd sort of way she almost felt sympathy for him.

'Do you still want me to continue working on the house?' she asked as he went to the door.

'You asked me that before,' he said with a hard stare, 'and the answer's still the same. Our personal relationship may have reached rock-bottom, but professionally, I still think you're the tops.'

The door closed quietly behind him, and Leslie was reminded of the day they had met, when she had been so rude to him and had expected him to slam it. But then, as now, he had kept his cool in the face of extreme provocation.

Perhaps a man who could keep his emotions under such tight control was incapable of the kind of love needed to commit himself to one woman. Maybe he had once been so badly hurt that the wall he had built around himself was impenetrable. If that were so, she had been wasting her time.

She slipped on her nightdress and clambered into bed. A host of questions continued to plague her, and as she finally drifted off to sleep, she still hadn't found a satisfactory answer to any of them.

CHAPTER SEVEN

THE following morning at breakfast, Leslie was not surprised to discover Dane had booked out of the hotel, and naturally his absence did not go unremarked.

'That was a short-lived reunion,' commented Marybeth, as she stretched out on a sunbed beside the pool. 'What went wrong?'

'The bedroom scene.'

'Don't tell me you didn't find it up to expectations?' Marybeth sounded incredulous.

'The dress rehearsal was great,' Leslie admitted, 'but I decided to cancel the opening night.'

'Having got that far, why, for heaven's sake?'

'Because I've always refused to sleep with him. I'm not interested in an affair. It's marriage or nothing.'

'Looks like you'll have to settle for nothing, then. From what you've told me, Dane's the original immovable object!'

It was a prophecy that proved all too true, for in the month that followed, Leslie neither saw nor heard from him. He avoided all his usual haunts, directives regarding the house were relayed via his secretary, and he made sure his visits never coincided with hers.

Yet each time the intercom buzzed in her office, or the phone rang in her apartment, she would momentarily expect to hear Dane's voice at the other end.

But she could not rely on feelings for ever, and gradually she started picking up the threads of her social life. A commission to design a clinic for a group of doctors introduced her to Grant Hayward, a heart specialist who lost no time in asking her out.

'Brains and beauty are an unusual mix in Tinsel Town,' he told her over drinks on their first date. 'How would you feel if I monopolised all your free evenings?'

'I might feel delighted.'

And she did. Divorced and childless, Grant was an attractive, intelligent man with whom she found it easy to relax. After the strain of the past months, when she continually had to watch her every word, it was refreshing to be her true self again.

She gained weight and the tension lines at the corners of her mouth and eyes disappeared. She eased off on her work-load too, and either spent the weekends at the beach, where Grant had a house, or on Robert's boat. Knowing how much she loved sailing, he had left it to her, as well as sufficient funds for its upkeep, which was considerable. Yet in the months since his death she had rarely taken it out, and had recently toyed with the idea of selling it.

But with Grant as her companion, the thirty-foot cabin cruiser roared into life again, and she spent many happy hours aboard, sunning, swimming and lazing, with the odd foray on water-skis. Though she was fairly proficient herself, Grant was the expert, and he soon had her jumping and balancing on one leg!

Yet in spite of his attractions she could not forget Dane. His image impinged on everything she did, until she began to wonder if her desire to teach him a lesson had turned into an obsessive mania. After all, she had tried her best to capture him and had failed, so why not call it a day and stop thinking about him?

More important, why couldn't she respond to the desire she saw so clearly in Grant's eyes?

'Come away with me one weekend?' His voice broke into her thoughts.

They were strolling along the beach in front of his house, hands lightly clasped. Tall, slim, and in his late thirties, he cut an athletic figure in a light grey tracksuit, the colour of his eyes.

'I wondered when you'd get around to that,' Leslie said ruefully.

'I was around it and back again the first night I met you!' Grant confessed. 'But I've been marking time. You're not the kind of girl who hops into bed just to say "thanks for a pleasant evening"!'

Leslie stopped walking and faced the sea, watching the light from the slowly setting sun cast its deep orange glow across the water. It was the time of day she loved best here, when the world seemed ringed with gold before the onrush of darkness.

'What would you say if I told you I'm not the sort of girl who hops into bed, period?'

'I'd say you were even more unique than I'd thought!'

'Unique good, or unique bad?'

He chuckled. 'Let's just say it won't stop me seeing you. Sex is important to me, but I'm willing to wait until you're ready.'

If only she knew when that would be! But if she went on feeling so despondent . . . She bit back a sigh, not knowing where it came from, or how to fight it.

'You're a nice man, Grant, and you deserve the answer you want. But at the moment I'm so muddled emotionally I can't think straight.'

'I gathered that. Someone mentioned you'd been dating Dane Jordan.'

'Yes, I was.' A tremor vibrated through her. 'But we——'

'You don't have to explain anything to me,' Grant silenced her. 'I'm a heart specialist, remember? And I'm expert at mending broken ones! In your case I'm even prepared to waive my very considerable fee!'

Leslie couldn't help smiling. 'Sounds like an offer I can't refuse.'

'Well then ...' He moved in on her, but she sidestepped.

'No, Grant, don't rush me. And don't raise your hopes either. I need time to come to myself; to know where I'm at, emotionally.'

'Keeping in a cocoon won't help you find out.'

'Nor will rushing into another relationship.'

'You really got hurt by Jordan, didn't you?' observed Grant.

'No. I hurt myself.'

And it was true. Blinded by the urge to take revenge, she had acted against her character, and was paying the price.

'Do you still love the guy?' asked Grant.

'I *never* loved him,' she stated vehemently. 'I had an obsession about him, but I'm gradually coming out of it.' She paused, wanting to explain why she had dated Dane, yet somehow reluctant to discuss her stepfather and the ugly events surrounding his stroke.

'One day I'll tell you the whole story, Grant. But for the moment I'd like to leave things as they are. I don't honestly know how I'll feel in the future and I'd be lying if I said I did.'

'But you enjoy being with me?'

'Of course I do. You're marvellous company.'

'And I have excellent references as a lover,' he said with mock solemnity. 'As a heart specialist, I'd like to prescribe some gentle treatment right away!'

'You're the doctor,' she said slowly, and made every effort to lose herself in his embrace as he drew her into his arms and pressed his mouth on hers.

He was as expert at kissing as at water-skiing, his touch confident, his hands soft but insidious, and knowing how to arouse. But she might as well have been a fish on a slab for all the response she felt, though she did her best to hide it.

It was well after midnight when they finally returned to her apartment. It was Sunday, and they arranged to have dinner together on Tuesday.

'My partners want to meet you during the week to discuss some changes to the ground floor of the clinic,' Grant said as he escorted her to her front door. 'If your secretary could call mine to arrange it . . .'

'I'll get her to do it first thing tomorrow,' Leslie promised. 'Thanks for a lovely weekend, Grant. You've been wonderfully understanding.'

'Something special's always worth waiting for, my darling, and I'm a patient man.' He smoothed her tousled hair, his fingers lingering on the curve of her cheek as he looked into her eyes. 'These past weeks have been the happiest since my divorce. I never thought I'd want to remarry, but we'd be good together, Leslie. We'd make a fine team.' She parted her lips to speak, but his thumb came across them to stop her. 'I know what you said earlier this evening, and I promise not to rush you.'

Not waiting for her reply, he strode away.

It was a pity Grant hadn't left things as they were, she thought as she undressed. Staving off an affair was not the same as allowing him to hope she might eventually marry him. But until her mind was totally free of Dane, she couldn't even begin to consider any kind of relationship with another man.

The door-bell cut across her thoughts, and she gave a nervous start. Who could it be at this hour of the morning? Grant returning? She didn't think it likely. Probably someone mistaking her apartment for the one opposite. It wouldn't be the first time either. The girl living there had a string of boy-friends who called at all hours.

But this time Leslie was wrong. Peering through the spyhole, she was stunned to see the unmistakable figure of Dane.

Leaving the safety chain on, she opened the door. Her heart lurched at the sight of him. He was unshaven and looked tired, his skin flushed as though he had been drinking. Not enough to lose control, perhaps, but enough to warn her to tread warily. Had he discovered she was Robert Webb's stepdaughter and put two and two together? Her heart beat faster.

'I've been trying to reach you since Friday,' he said without preamble. 'Where the hell have you been all weekend?'

'I don't think that's any of your business.' She kept her tone mild. 'Don't you think it's rather late to be calling on someone?'

'No, I don't.' He rattled the chain. 'Undo this damn thing and let me in!'

'I don't make a habit of seeing clients after office hours.'

'You know damn well I'm not here to discuss work!'

'Really? When I last saw you, you said we'd nothing left to discuss on a *personal* level.'

'I'm in no mood for games, he exploded. 'Open the door!'

Resignedly she did. Dane was spoiling for a fight, and short of having one on her front doorstep . . .

'I won't offer you a nightcap, as you've clearly had several already.' She switched on the living-room lights. 'But I can make you some black coffee.'

'No, thanks.'

'OK. It's your hangover, not mine.'

'You're bloody well responsible for my condition!'

The sharp edge in his voice warned her she was treading on dangerous ground, but she was becoming too weary to care. 'Indeed?'

'Yes, indeed. I've been sitting in my car the whole evening waiting for you to come back, and it whiled away the hours.'

'Try a good book next time,' she said coldly.

'There won't be a next time, Leslie. From now on *I'll* be bringing you home.' Glinting eyes, almost black, showed the temper he was controlling, as did the thick eyebrows drawn together in a frown. 'Who was the man you were with, and what does he mean to you?'

So that was it! He was jealous again! She hid her elation and spoke in a deliberately casual tone. 'His name's Grant Hayward, and he's a heart specialist.'

'An old friend or a new one?'

'New.'

'You're on pretty intimate terms for a short acquaintance.'

'I don't know what you mean by intimate,' she shrugged.

'I watched him pawing you at the door before he left.'

'Peeping Tom, are you?'

'I was waiting at the end of the corridor,' Dane bit out. 'Didn't take you long to get over me, did it?'

'Is that what bugs you—that I'm not staying home pining for you? I'm a realist, Dane, and you made your feelings quite clear at La Costa.'

'So it's off with the old and on with the new?'

'Grant's a friend, nothing more.'

'So what were you two friends up to all weekend? Talking?'

'Yes, surprising as that may seem to you. We happen to have a lot in common.'

Suddenly weary of Dane's hectoring—last time his jealousy had only led to a sexual impasse, and this would no doubt end in the same manner—Leslie turned away.

'For heaven's sake get out of here and leave me alone. I've nothing more to say to you.'

'But I've plenty to say to you!'

His hands shot out and gripped her, spinning her round to face him. The wildness in his eyes showed that his anger came from more than pique, and, frightened, she tried to pull free.

'Don't worry,' he said grimly, 'I won't wring your neck, though there's nothing I'd like better. If you knew the hell you've put me through this month!'

'Hell? Why, I've done everything possible to keep out of your hair!'

'That's what's driven me mad! I'd hoped that by not seeing you I'd forget you—but it hasn't worked out that way—the opposite, in fact!'

Leslie's elation grew as it dawned on her that at long last, when she had settled for failure, her scheming was coming to fruition.

'I can't sleep, I can't eat, and I can't even look at another woman!' Dane went on, making it sound like the eighth wonder of the world. 'You win, Leslie. If there's only one way I can have you, then that's what it'll have to be.' His voice sank so low it was barely audible. 'Will you marry me?'

Leslie felt drunk with triumph. She had achieved

the impossible; toppled the most virulent champion of Men's Lib! From tonight, the cause of bachelordom had received a blow from which it might never recover.

'You're asking me to *marry* you?'

'Do you want me to repeat it so you can have your pound of flesh all over again? Yes, Leslie, I'm asking you to be my wife. And if you refuse, I'll make your life hell till you agree!'

'Put like that, how can I say no?' she said huskily, re-thinking herself into the role she had created, which she would have to play for the foreseeable future. 'Yes, yes, yes, my darling! Just name the day and I'll be yours!'

With a shaky, indrawn breath, Dane wrapped his arms around her, the relief on his face so palpable it told her how scared he had been he might have lost her. His next words confirmed it.

'When I found you'd gone away for the weekend, and then saw that guy bringing you back tonight, saw the way he looked at you and kissed you, I thought I'd left it too late.'

Leslie almost felt sorry for him. Knowing him as she did, she knew what it had cost him to propose marriage. Not that he had actually burnt his boats proper and admitted he loved her, though it was implicit in his every action.

Winding her arms around his neck, she caressed the nape and ran her fingers through his thick, silky hair in a gesture of understanding. His response was immediate, and he claimed her lips with a passion that was all-consuming, as if wanting to absorb her into the very fibre of his being. Urgently he tore apart the fastening of her dress, which slithered to the floor, leaving her naked except for brief lace panties.

Automatically she went to cover her breasts, but he caught her hands and drew them to his throat.

'Don't fight me,' he said thickly. 'Don't stop me tonight.' He crushed her to him, his hardness throbbingly alive as he moved against her. 'Touch me, sweetheart, make love . . . hold me . . .' he said jerkily, and lowered her hands to his body.

Through the soft tangle of his hair, Leslie felt the dampness of his skin, the wild throbbing of his desire. It was a pulsating virility she couldn't resist, and it carried her on a wave of passion as powerful as his.

Recognising her surrender, he began kissing her again, prising her lips apart, loving her with his tongue.

'I want you so much, darling,' he breathed against her mouth.

Deftly he lowered her to the couch and shrugged free of his clothes. The almost imperceptible sound of his trouser-zip rang a deafening warning in her ears, and with a cry she jumped up and put the length of the settee between them. Was Dane playing her for a fool? Was his proposal a cheap trick to get her into bed? If so, she would call his bluff.

'I can't!' she cried, retrieving her dress and hurriedly slipping it on. 'I've told you before, Dane. Not until we're married.'

Dumbfounded, he stared at her. 'Don't you trust me?'

'Of course I do,' she said, but felt her cheeks redden.

'Liar,' he murmured, but it was not said angrily. Indeed a rueful smile moved his mouth. 'You're wrong about me, you know. If I could I'd marry you tonight, this minute.'

Momentarily, Leslie was disconcerted, for his sincerity was palpable.

'I-I'm sorry, Dane. It's just that after all the things you've said in the past, I find it hard to believe you really love me.'

'But I don't,' he announced smoothly, 'and I won't pretend I do. I desire you, ache for you, but I don't love you. I'm marrying you because I can't have you any other way. It doesn't mean our marriage has less chance of being successful. In fact the odds are probably better for us. Apart from wanting you like crazy, I enjoy your company and admire your brain.'

Leslie, trying to act like the girl she was pretending to be, wondered if she should ask for time to think things over. Or would a truly adoring doormat be willing to accept him on any terms?

'Well?' he said. 'You're not normally stuck for a reply.'

'This isn't a normal situation.'

'I guess it isn't. I'm sorry I can't declare undying love, but I won't enter this relationship on a lie. You have my friendship and respect, and I hope that's enough. Many marriages have succeeded on far less.'

'You're very convincing, Dane,' she told him softly.

'Does that mean "yes"?'

She nodded. 'But only on condition that you don't try to get me into bed until our wedding day.'

'What about a sofa, or the floor?'

'Don't be funny!'

'Who's being funny? I'm willing to take you any time, any place.'

'Stop it!'

'OK.' His smile was wry. 'I'll agree to your demands. But for my clients' sake at least, set the date soon!' He pulled her into his arms again. 'From experience, I can tell you that abstinence doesn't make the heart grow fonder. All it does is play havoc with one's concentration!'

'So will lack of sleep,' she answered, her green eyes wide. 'Do you know the time?'

'Nearer dawn than midnight. But at least give me a kiss before you throw me out.' He bent and placed his lips on hers, then moved them across her cheek and temple before finding her mouth again. 'Until tomorrow, my sweetheart,' he murmured, drawing away with reluctance. 'We'll go down to City Hall to see about the licence. Then if you're free for lunch, we'll discuss wedding plans.'

'I'll make myself free. From now on, you take priority over everyone and everything.'

'I'll double that in diamonds,' he responded humorously. 'At Tiffany's, in fact, to pick out your engagement ring.'

'You don't waste time, do you?'

'I've a lot to make up,' he said huskily, and putting her away from him, walked briskly out.

Leslie leaned against the door for several seconds. Then switching off the lights, she went into her bedroom. She couldn't understand why she no longer felt elated. On the contrary, she was decidedly depressed. Yet why? After all, she had achieved what she had set out to do. She hadn't been able to make him fall in love with her, of course, but that was the nature of the man rather than a fault within herself— and if anything, could be regarded as a plus. For knowing he was marrying her for physical reasons alone would stop her having any pangs of conscience when she eventually left him.

It was not until many months later that she had cause to question why she should have had a conscience about Dane anyway—and by then, it was too late for regrets.

CHAPTER EIGHT

As Leslie had anticipated, the news of Dane's impending marriage caused quite a stir, the media affording it the coverage normally reserved for pop-stars and mass murders. They were bombarded with requests for interviews, and even private occasions became public as journalists and photographers trailed them wherever they went.

Instant fame as Dane's fiancée was not a bit to Leslie's liking. Indeed fame on any level had never appealed to her. Success in her chosen field, and admiration by her peers, was all she desired. Yet now she found herself a public figure, gawped at and treated with awe simply because she was going to marry the most famous divorce lawyer in the States.

'I'm surprised you don't enjoy all the fuss,' said Dane, when she voiced her distaste. 'Most of the women I know would give their eye teeth for it.'

'Most of the women you know have only one thought in their heads,' she retorted. 'To catch a rich husband.'

'Don't knock them, honey. They do the best with what they have which is basically what we all do.'

Leslie made a face at him. 'I should know better than to argue with a litigious lawyer!'

'Can I take it you'll become a yes-woman?'

'Is that what you'd like?'

'Heaven forbid! A meek little *hausfrau* would bore me out of my skull.'

Leslie stored this away along with several other

interesting titbits he had let slip, knowing it might come in useful in the months ahead.

'Most men like to be boss,' she said aloud. 'Even when they pay lip-service to equality.'

'I'm not most men,' he said good-naturedly. 'I practise what I preach.'

'How many women partners do you have in your firm?' she pounced.

'Not as many as I'd like.'

'You're evading the question.'

'I'm not, but we don't get all that number of female applicants anxious to specialise in divorce.'

'But all things being equal, would you be as happy to promote a woman as a man?'

'Certainly. Except that all things are rarely equal, are they?'

'You have a typical lawyer's habit of answering a question with a question,' she said irritably.

'It usually means the person can't think of an answer!' he chuckled.

'I'll remember that next time you do it!'

He chuckled again. 'I love riling you, darling. You rise to the bait so beautifully.'

'Well, I can't rise any more,' she said, glancing at her watch. 'I've an appointment, and I'm already late.'

He studied her for a moment, as if not sure she was speaking the truth, and she met his gaze unwaveringly. They were lunching at Jimmy's, a restaurant they favoured as much for the food as the fact that it was a half-way meeting place for them both.

'If you care to come with me,' she said, 'I'll prove it. It's at *your* house.'

'*Our* house,' he corrected. 'And I think I'll take you up on it.'

'Good. You haven't dropped by in almost a week, so

you'll see quite a few changes.'

'OK—you've called my bluff.' Dane gave a sheepish smile. 'I'm due in court at three—or did you already know?'

Leslie was both amused and irritated. 'You really *are* a suspicious man, aren't you?'

'Not suspicious—just jealous.'

'Pity. And here I was, thinking you perfect.'

'I practically am,' he said solemnly. 'Hardworking, kind to old ladies and dogs, and extremely patient where my fiancée's concerned.'

She knew instantly what he meant, and coloured. Since the night he had asked her to marry him, he had behaved like a brother! So much so that she had occasionally found herself wishing he would lose his self-control! She had never tried to deny that she found him physically attractive, and seeing him most evenings as she was doing, the pull of his personality was, if anything, becoming more magnetic. It was the danger-point of their relationship; the one weak link in her armour, and it scared her to death.

'If your patience holds out until our wedding night,' she quipped, 'you'll deserve a good conduct medal!'

'I hope I'll deserve more than that! I don't want to spend my honeymoon taking cold showers!'

'Not even together?' she suggested impishly.

He feigned horror. 'I see you being a very corrupting influence on me, Miss Watson.'

'Appearances can be deceptive, Mr Jordan.'

'I'll look forward to you proving it!' Dane reached across the table to clasp her hand. 'You wouldn't like to start now, would you?'

'I don't think the managment would approve.' Leslie glanced around the packed room. 'It might give the customers indigestion.'

Dane laughed, an uninhibited sound that drew the attention of neighbouring diners. 'I'd say a good deal more than indigestion, taking their ages into account!' he added, uncaring of the inquisitive stares he had attracted.

This was one of the things Leslie liked in him. Without being brash, he was supremely self-assured, an assurance that came from inner confidence rather than success.

'So I take it the answer's still no?' he questioned.

Her expression spoke for her as she pushed back her chair. 'What time shall I be ready this evening?' she asked, as they wended their way out.

'Eight, as we're the guests of honour. Caldwell wants us there early.'

While they waited for Leslie's car to be brought round by an attendant, they discussed tonight's party—one of many they had been invited to since their engagement. Dane had a wide circle of friends whose main preoccupation seemed to be competing with each other as to who was the most lavish host.

'I guess I'd better wear something long and glittery,' she murmured.

'Absolutely. Half the movie colony will be there, and you know how they love dressing up.'

But studying her wardrobe later that evening, Leslie decided against her most expensive dress—no way could she compete with women who spent thousands of dollars on a single garment—and the black satin Twenties dress she finally chose relied for its effect on style rather than cut and decoration, while the minimal bodice—supported by shoestring straps that criss-crossed the low-cut back—was the perfect foil for her creamy skin.

In keeping with the Twenties look, she twisted her

hair into a coil at the nape of her neck—the style enhancing the long sweep of her throat—and tied a black-beaded headband across her forehead. Her make-up fitted the era too, the soft contours of her mouth outlined with deep red lip-gloss, her slanting eyes shaded with shimmering silver-gilt.

Surveying herself in one of the mirrors that lined her wall-to-wall bedroom cupboards, Leslie clipped on the single strand of pearls that had been a graduation gift from her stepfather. Seeing them gleaming upon her skin brought back such poignant memories of him that it reaffirmed her determination to continue the path she was treading.

She had grown too soft towards Dane these past few weeks; had allowed the sharp edges of her dislike to be dulled by the intimacy of their new found relationship. Her cheeks burned with shame. It was no good running away from the fact that she had allowed his charismatic personality to seduce her. He was so stimulating that every other man paled into insignificance by comparison.

Once again she was assailed by fear, realising that the longer she stayed with him the more she would come under his spell, and the harder it would be to extricate herself when the time came for her to leave him.

The house-phone buzzed three times—a prearranged signal—and she reached for her purse, casually looped a fringed silk shawl across her shoulders, and went downstairs, her vampish appearance giving no hint of the dark mood it concealed.

Dane was waiting beside his Rolls convertible, the hood down in the unusually balmy October evening. He looked so devastatingly handsome in his dinner-jacket that her pulses jumped nervously, but she managed to hide it as she slid into the seat beside him.

His expression told her she had had the same impact on him, though unlike her he verbalised it. 'You're absolutely stunning, darling. You make it dammed hard for a man to concentrate his thoughts on a higher plane!'

'You like my dress, then?' she purred.

'I like what's in it! Every woman at the party will gnash her caps with envy!'

'I doubt that.'

'Stop being falsely modest. You know you're beautiful.'

'Beautiful girls are a dime a dozen in this town. So why should I feel special?'

'You're special to me—which is all that counts,' he said, lifting her fingers to his lips

'Watch the red light!' she warned, and used the opportunity to retrieve her hand. Disturbed by his touch as much as by his words, she spoke more sharply than she had intended, and he gave her a quizzical glance.

'You sound just like a wife! I hope you won't turn into a nag once we're hitched.'

'It's perfectly natural for me to change a bit,' she answered. 'And so will you.'

'You're perfect as you are.'

'Your mind's stuck in one groove today!' she teased.

'Not only today! But as long as I stick to words and not actions, you can't complain!' He shot her another glance. 'How do you like my jacket? I had it flown over from London.'

'It's very nice.'

'Can't you do better than that?'

'Sure. But I won't. You're conceited enough as it is.'

'You're doing your best to knock it out of me,' he

said wryly. 'You seem to enjoy putting me down.'

'Your friends don't think so. I bore them to tears singing your praises.'

'I wouldn't mind you doing a bit of trilling in *my* ear. As we only make verbal love, it would be nice if it wasn't entirely one-sided!'

Though his tone was jocular, Leslie recognised the serious undertone in it.

'I'm sorry, darling,' she apologised with all the sincerity she could muster. 'I suppose I thought that playing it cool would make it easier for you.'

'There's a difference between cool and cold. And at times your well-intentioned little blasts are positively arctic!'

She lifted her hand to caress his cheek gently. 'It's a difficult time for both of us, Dane. But the warm winds of summer are only three weeks away!'

Her reference to their wedding instantly restored his good humour. 'From then on,' he said happily, 'may all our clouds be little ones! I'll leave you to decide how many.'

A hot tide of embarrassment swept across her body, and agitatedly she twisted her engagement ring—a pear-shaped diamond that had set Dane back a king's ransom.

'I thought you didn't want children,' she murmured.

'I've changed my mind—and not just about that, but a lot of other things too.'

'Such as?'

'I'll tell you when we're married.'

'What's wrong with now?' she pressed. 'Why the secrecy?'

He shook his head and her curiosity grew.

'Give me a hint, Dane. If whatever it is falls through, I promise I won't be disappointed.'

He laughed. 'Only a woman would make such a ridiculous promise and expect it to be taken seriously!'

'And only a man wouldn't realise that once a woman's curiosity is aroused, she won't rest until it's satisfied! It's tantamount to cruelty.'

'So sue me!'

'Know a good, cheap lawyer?'

'I know one who'll take his fee in kind, for a good-looking chick like you!'

'How unethical!'

'You're worth my being disbarred—and hell, we can always live on *your* salary!'

'Not in a two-million-dollar home we can't! We'd have to come down in the world and move into my apartment.'

Dane swung into the driveway of a mock-Tudor mansion, and was directed to a parking-space by a security guard, one of several in evidence about the property.

'I'll only tell you when I'm ready,' said Dane, referring to their previous conversation as he drew the Rolls to a halt.

Their eyes met, laughter in both, yet something deeper flickering in his that Leslie could not fathom.

'You're impossible, Dane Jordan!' she smiled.

'And you're adorable. I hope the girls take after you!'

His hand clasping hers, they approached the baronial entrance, and the sound of a string orchestra playing a Strauss waltz wafted out to them.

'That has to be the Los Angeles Symphony,' Leslie commented.

'Spot on,' he agreed. 'And they just come with the hors d'oeuvre!'

He wasn't joking either. By the time dancing

commenced in the floodlit garden, on a floor constructed alongside the Grecian-styled pool, there had been two more changes of orchestra, each as famous as its predecessor.

'All that's missing is Frank Sinatra,' a movie star commented as he wirled Leslie around the floor. 'Caldwell's thought of everything else!'

How right he was! Dom Perignon champagne flowed like Perrier water, and the buffet table was weighed down with Beluga caviar, Maine lobsters and *foie gras*.

Yet despite the glamour and glitter, Leslie felt no regret that her life among the rich and famous would be brief. She had nothing in common with the pampered, spoiled women who were more sheen than substance, or the men who talked money in telephone numbers, and paid scant attention to the world outside it. But she kept her opinions to herself, for she saw Dane was totally at ease among them, and there was no denying the high regard in which they held him.

'Why so pensive?' he asked as they relaxed on their own on one of the hammocks dotting the pool area.

'I'm thinking of our wedding,' she lied. 'It'll be pretty tame compared with this.'

'We agreed it should be small and private. But if you want something bigger . . .'

She was surprised by his willingness to give in to her. 'I didn't mean it enviously, Dane. I merely wondered whether your friends would be disappointed.'

'I'm marrying you, not my friends. It's what *you* want that counts.'

'Ah, the love-birds!'

The Southern drawl came from their host, who hailed from North Carolina, as did his third wife, a redhead of statuesque proportions, thirty years his junior. Caldwell Mather was in his mid-fifties but looked younger, his craggy face not unattractive.

'Not opting out already?' he chided. 'The party's just beginning.'

'Not everyone has your stamina,' Dane quipped.

'Does that mean you aren't going to dance with me?' Beverly Mather cooed, twining her arm through Dane's. 'You've neglected me all evening.'

'I'll make amends now,' he replied instantly, and led her to the dance-floor, closely followed by Leslie and her host.

It was nearly an hour later before Leslie met up with Dane again, for they had both had several partners cutting in on them.

'Do you think we can leave?' she murmured. 'I'm out on my feet.'

'Me too. But I'd like to wait a while longer. It would be rude if we left before midnight.'

Leslie conceded, though dropping with exhaustion. It was their third late night in succession, and this, together with a hectic work schedule—she was attempting to sort out several problems before her wedding day—was beginning to tell on her.

'Will we see you before the big day?' Caldwell asked Dane when they finally said goodnight.

'I'm not sure.'

'Why don't we have lunch together?' Beverly suggested to Leslie in an aside.

'Mind if I take a raincheck?' Leslie feigned regret. 'If I don't clear my desk, Dane will have to honeymoon alone!'

'You're not working after you're married, are you?' Cornflower-blue eyes regarded her with astonishment. 'Why not relax and have fun?'

'My work's my fun.'

'Won't Dane mind your being busy the whole time?'

'Too bad if he does. He asked Leslie Watson, architect, to marry him, with no conditions attached.'

'Dane mentioned that you can be pretty determined,' the girl commented admiringly.

'So can he,' Leslie smiled. 'And it's made for some stormy passages!'

'Arguments are good for a relationship—they give you insight into a person's character. It's hard to maintain a phoney persona if you're throwing an ashtray!'

Leslie stared at Beverly, who grinned broadly.

'I'm not quite as dumb as I look,' the girl continued. 'Caldwell likes to think of me as the little woman, so I play along with him! But I majored in psychology, you know, though you mustn't breathe a word to him!'

'I promise. But you amaze me. Surely Caldwell would be proud of your achievements?'

'Don't you believe it! He's a bright guy, but he never got to college, so he has a complex about it. But that's his only hang-up and I'm happy to pander to it.'

'Don't you resent having to act dumb?' queried Leslie.

'Not if it preserves my marriage.' Beverly looked round to ensure the men were still out of earshot. 'I come from a dirt-poor family and was determined to have some security when I married. When Caldwell came along, I didn't hesitate. I'd have liked someone like Dane, who appreciated brains as well as beauty, but I couldn't find someone, so I settled for second best.'

'With no regrets?'

'Only when I meet a girl who has it all—like you!' Beverly's warm smile showed she wasn't being bitchy.

'I hope we can be friends, Leslie. It would be nice having someone with whom I can be my real self.'

Leslie knew what she meant, and felt an unexpected pang of sympathy for the girl. Beverly was an accomplished hostess, a faithful wife, according to Dane, and an adoring mother to her one-year-old daughter. What a pity she had to hide her intellect.

'We'll have lunch as soon as I get back from honeymoon,' she promised. 'I'm really tied up for the next few weeks.'

On the drive home, she told Dane the gist of her conversation with Beverly, curious to know if he had suspected there was more to the girl than met the eye.

'As a matter of fact I did,' he said. 'I've dealt with too many women not to recognise the difference between playing dumb and being dumb.'

'But Caldwell's no fool. How come *he* hasn't guessed?'

'Love is blind.'

Did this apply to Dane too? Leslie mused. Yet he had said quite categorically he wasn't in love with her!

'Perhaps it's the reason I think *you're* perfect,' she said sweetly.

He laughed. 'Only my mother thinks that!'

'Talking of your mother,' Leslie decided a change of subject was called for, 'when do you expect her?' Mrs Jordan had written to her warmly on learning of their engagement, and had promised to spend a few days with them before the wedding.

'Damn! I meant to tell you.' Dane shook his head. 'She called this morning to say she can't be at the wedding. She's leaving for Jeddah first thing tomorrow. Cathy's had a fall and could lose the baby.'

Dane's sister lived in Saudi Arabia with her oil executive husband, and after bringing up three children, had unexpectedly become pregnant on her fortieth birthday.

'She wants my mother with her till she's over the worst,' he explained.

Leslie was relieved not to be meeting Mrs Jordan. Feigning the adoring fiancée in front of his friends was one thing; fooling his mother could have been much more difficult.

'I'm sorry I won't be meeting her,' Leslie lied. 'I was looking forward to it.'

'So was she. She despaired of me ever marrying, and now having to miss it . . .' He drew to a stop outside the apartment block. 'I was thinking of having a video made of our wedding and sending it out to her.'

'A lovely idea!' Leslie forced enthusiasm. 'How thoughtful you are.'

'No more than most sons.' He shrugged off the compliment.

'I'll drop your mother a note,' Leslie said. 'I didn't answer her letter because I thought I'd be seeing her.'

'Phone me at the office for Cathy's address. My memory isn't too good lately.'

'As long as you remember to turn up for our wedding!'

'The date's blazoned on my heart,' he flashed. 'It's the biggest step of my life.'

And one you'll live to regret, Leslie vowed silently, as she gave him her most innocent smile and most loving goodnight kiss.

CHAPTER NINE

MUCH as Leslie had dreaded her wedding day, when it finally came she found herself enjoying it, caught up in the excitement generated by family and friends, as well as Dane's uninhibited pleasure. In fact he exuded so much bonhomie that not even the crowds of stargazers, photographers and reporters lying in wait for them outside the town hall could rattle him.

Later, at the luncheon they gave at The Hermitage, he rarely took his eyes from her face or his hand from her waist. For someone who wasn't in love he gave a good pretence of it, and though the gestures might only have been possessive ones, she found his touch sensual and exciting, leaving her in no doubt that however resolute her mind, her body would betray her.

'Happy?' he whispered in her ear, after they had cut the wedding cake.

'Ecstatically,' she whispered back. 'I'm frightened I'll wake up and find it's all a dream.'

'You look like one. Or have I told you that already?'

'Not for the past five minutes!'

'Break it up you two!' This from the youngest of Dane's sisters. 'You're melting the icing!'

Everyone laughed, and the band struck up 'People Will Say We're In Love', which resulted in even more merriment—though not from Leslie, who was all too conscious of the irony of it.

Three hours later they were winging their way to Europe, first stop London. Weather-wise it wasn't a clever choice for November, but when Dane had suggested Barbados or Bali, Leslie had vetoed it. Sunlit days and moonlit nights were settings for true lovers, not those playing at it—but naturally she hadn't given that as her reason, saying instead that they needed furnishings for their house, and it would be fun to combine their honeymoon with a buying trip.

'Traipsing around stores is hardly my idea of a romantic honeymoon,' he had protested.

'I know, darling. But I'd planned on getting several things for the house in Europe, and if you weren't able to come with me . . .' Tantalisingly she dangled their separation as bait. 'We need only spend a few days in London and Milan,' she pointed out, 'then we can go on to Venice. I hear it's the loveliest city in the world.'

'It is,' he had said happily, and had added Paris to their itinerary, extending their absence to four weeks instead of three.

'I'm surprised you can take so much time off,' she remarked as they sat sipping champagne in the upstairs lounge of the aircraft. 'I thought you were in the middle of preparing a big case.'

'I am.' He nodded towards the crocodile briefcase beside him on the floor. 'However busy you keep me, I'm hoping to snatch a little time to look over it.'

The implication was obvious, and colour suffused her cheeks. Quickly she glanced away.

'I love it when you blush,' he said softly.

'I suppose you find it amusing.' She looked back at him. 'Especially at my age.'

'I'm not poking fun at you, sweetheart. I'm sorry if it came out that way. Your innocence is a bonus, Leslie. I'm going to enjoy teaching you the art of love.'

'Love*making*,' she corrected stonily. 'There's a difference.'

'You're splitting hairs.'

'Yes. But you get my meaning.'

'Indeed I do. But it's rather late to be having second thoughts. We're married now, for better or worse.'

'Would you force yourself on me?' Leslie blurted out.

Dane was startled, as if the idea had never occurred to him. 'Of course not. There's no satisfaction making love to a statue.' Setting down his glass, he took her hand, his skin warm against the cold of hers. 'Look, darling, I'm not sure what you're trying to tell me, but any fears you have are nothing more than first-night nerves.'

'It's more than that.' Her voice was ragged. 'Maybe I don't relish the prospect of sleeping with a man who doesn't love me.'

'There are degrees of love,' he said with such reasonableness that she knew there was no way she could carry on her argument. 'If your previous reaction to my lovemaking is anything to go by, I don't envisage any problems.'

Leslie sighed inwardly. The trouble was, neither did she. It had been a forlorn hope to imagine she could provoke him into forgoing his marital rights.

'In fact, I only hope I can keep up with you,' he went on. 'According to the sex books, you're in your prime and I'm past it!'

'Is that why you've been stoking up with oysters?'

'Naturally. And crocodiles' teeth under my pillow as a talisman!'

It was mid-morning when they landed at Heathrow, but despite the sun shining brightly in a clear blue sky, there was an undoubted nip in the air, and Leslie shivered despite her heavy tweed suit.

'This is fur coat weather,' said Dane, noticing.

'We'll look around for one tomorrow.'

'I've brought a mink jacket.'

'That won't be warm enough.'

'I've a camel coat too.'

'Not my favourite animal,' he teased. 'I'd prefer you in sable.'

'I've managed quite well without one.'

'You've also managed quite well without expensive jewellery and couture clothes—but I expect my wife to have them.' He steadied her with his hand as their taxi careered round a corner. 'And don't say you're not like most Hollywood wives, because I know that already. It's why I married you, remember?'

'As long as *you* remember it.'

'Always, my darling. But I'm still getting you a fur coat!'

Knowing when she was beaten, Leslie fell silent. She was Dane's wife and had to play the game his way—for the moment.

They reached the hotel, and a porter came forward to help her from the taxi. Though this wasn't her first time in London, it was a totally new experience for her to stay at Claridges. Previously she had slummed it in South Kensington!

'Like it?' Dane enquired, as a bellboy deposited their luggage in a magnificent flower-filled suite, and they were alone once more.

'It's OK,' she shrugged, then giggled as she saw his expression. 'Don't be silly, darling! It's absolutely fabulous.'

'Not too Beverly Hills for you?' he teased. 'What would you say if I told you Liz Taylor once stayed in this suite?'

'I'd say it won't kill me to live like a movie star for a few days!' Leslie's eyes ranged over the exquisite sitting-room. 'Do you always stay here when you're in London?'

'Not these particular rooms. I generally fly in at short notice and take what's available. But this trip I moved heaven and earth—or at least a minor European Royal—to get it for you.'

Leslie couldn't help wondering if Dane had brought other women here, and was surprised how disturbing she found the idea.

'No, Mrs Jordan of the ingenuous face, I've never stayed here with another woman,' he said, reading her mind with uncanny accuracy, and more than a hint of amusement.

'You can't blame me for wondering.'

'Think I'd be so insensitive?'

She shrugged, and watched as he leafed through the pile of messages left for him on the gilt and walnut bureau. 'Not business, I hope?'

'No. Most are congratulatory letters from English colleagues, and four are from newspapers and TV chat shows asking for interviews.'

'What it is to be famous!'

He laughed. 'They only want to talk to me because I got married. I'm the man who's supposed to be against it.'

'How will you explain your change of heart?'

'I'll show them you!' He dropped the letters back on the bureau. 'I'll probably do a couple of interviews and one chat show—no more than that.'

Curiously deflated by his need for ego-boosting, Leslie said, 'Do you enjoy being a celebrity, Dane?'

'Not much. But it's good for my practice. Every time I get publicity, Jordan Associates picks up new clients. And not only divorce cases—that's just my side of it—but anything from libel to larceny.'

'Does that mean you'll be doing shows everywhere we go?'

'I'll scrap them all if you'd prefer. This is our honeymoon, and you come first.'

'Are you sure you can afford the sacrifice?'

'Spending my time with you is no sacrifice,' he said easily, choosing to ignore her irony. He moved to the bar, where a bottle of champagne nestled in a silver ice-bucket. 'A drink, sweetheart?'

'I'll take a bath first. I need freshening up.' She yawned to emphasise the point. 'I didn't get much sleep last night, and unlike you, I couldn't make it up on the plane.'

'A bath sounds a good idea,' he agreed. 'I'll have one too.'

'When do we eat?' she asked, glancing at her watch.

Not that she had any appetite. Like taking a bath, the suggestion was simply another delaying tactic. And as senseless, she realised, for she could not put off the inevitable for ever.

'We'll eat whenever you want,' he answered her. 'But to be honest I'm only ravenous for *you*.'

'I—er—wouldn't you prefer to wait until—er——'

'Don't be embarrassed, darling,' he cut in softly. 'I've waited so long, I'm sure I can last till you've satisfied your hunger pangs! I'll get room-service to send up something. What would you like?'

'Fish. I'll leave the choice to you.'

'Deciding to let Dane bath first, so that she could unpack and hang out the creases in her clothes, she thought it would be a wifely gesture to do his unpacking too, and had just put away the last of his things when he returned to the bedroom.

His hair was still damp and gleamed like black satin, and there was a scrubbed, fresh look about him that made it hard for her to equate him with the cold, storming man she had first seen across a courtroom a year ago. A short navy towelling robe was tied loosely around his waist, and aware of his nakedness beneath it, she had to force herself not to look away. She was a mature young woman, for heaven's sake, and had already seen Dane in the nude! Remembering how that particular episode had ended, and knowing this one would end far differently, she felt warm colour suffuse her face.

'I've—er—unpacked for you,' she said jerkily.

'So I see. That was kind of you, darling.' He eyed the tidy room. 'I see you've an orderly mind, like me.'

'I hope that means you squeeze the toothpaste from the bottom up!' She was glad to make a joke.

'We can have separate tubes, if you like.'

'Start with separate tubes, and you can never tell where it will end!' Leslie headed towards the bathroom, hoping he hadn't mistaken 'tube' for 'tub'. That was one particular intimacy she wasn't ready for!

But again she had misjudged him, for he didn't even come into the bathroom. That he wanted her desperately was obvious, but not with the crass passion of a boy. Dane was a sophisticated man, and knew he had to persuade her into submission, not claim possession by right.

She lingered as long as was reasonable in the scented water—Rochas' Mystère, with the compliments of the management—then reached for her bathcoat.

Catching sight of her reflection as she wrapped it around her, she was unexpectedly reminded of Bonnard's 'Nude before the Mirror'. With her shiny face, streaked blonde hair piled in loose abandon atop her head, and well proportioned figure, pink and glowing from the water, she could well have been his model. Maybe a few extra pounds to her slender frame would give a better likeness, she decided critically, and pulled back her shoulders, The provocative pose gave an alluring tilt to her breasts, and her mind returned instantly to Dane. Tonight he would be fondling them, rousing them to a tingling awareness, plundering her depths as no other man had done; exploring the most intimate parts of her body as she placed his seal of possession on her.

Trembling, she rubbed herself dry and slipped on her nightdress and matching négligé. They did little to dispel her wayward thoughts, for the fine white silk and lace gave her skin the lustre of magnolia blossom, and outlined the curves of her body as clearly as if she had been naked. Enough to raise the blood presure of any man, she thought without conceit, but wasted on Dane, for his was already at boiling point.

Resisting the urge to slip back into her towelling robe, she went into the sitting-room. Wryly she saw he hadn't wasted any time. The overhead lighting had been switched off and the lamps dimmed to a soft glow. The soft strains of James Last provided background music at a romantic range of decibels, while the bridegroom himself lounged indolently against the bar, appraising his bride with warm brown eyes. In cream silk pyjamas, piped in navy, and a matching navy and white dressing-gown, he looked utterly at ease. And why not? This wasn't the first time he had been in such a situation—though it was the first time the woman had had his ring on her finger!

'I'm ready for my champagne now,' she said, trying to keep her voice steady.

'Your wish is my command.' Effortlessly uncorking a bottle, he filled two glasses.

'To us,' he toasted, 'and the beginning of a wonderful life.'

Leslie touched her glass to his, and they both took a sip.

'Hope that didn't sound too trite?' Dane said.

'Triteness, like clichés, is often the best way of expressing oneself.'

'I'm glad you think so, because here stands the king of clichés. I use loads of them when I sum up in court!'

Leslie longed to say she knew it only too well, but stopped herself.

The arrival of dinner provided a welcome interruption to her thoughts, and while Dane refilled their glasses, she lifted the silver covers off the first course, a creamy lobster bisque. Though she knew it had to be delicious, it tasted like sawdust to her, and it was all she could do to pretend she was enjoying it.

Dane, on the other hand, ate with blithe unconcern, keeping up a constant patter of trivia, and seemingly not noticing her monosyllabic replies. If his intention was to take her mind off the coming night, he was having little success, for her attention kept wandering to the half-open bedroom door and the king-size bed, its satin cover turned down in readiness.

'More champagne?' he enquired, watching her divide the strawberries Romanoff between them.

'No, thanks. I've had more than enough.'

'Food too?' he asked, seeing her toy with her dessert. 'Or shall I order you something else?'

'This is fine, I'm full, that's all.'

'How about some exercise to help the digestion? And I don't mean what you think I mean!' he added. 'I was simply suggesting we dance.'

'Why not?' she said, and wondered if it was another of his ploys to help her relax! Poor Dane, she thought, as he drew her into his arms. I must be the only girl he's actually had to push to bed—the others all jumped.

The strains of Sinatra singing 'Easy to Love' acted on her hypnotically, and she rested her cheek on Dane's. Then finding it difficult to move on the thick carpet in heels, she kicked of her white satin mules.

'That's better,' he murmured, drawing her head to his shoulder. 'Much, much better.'

As he drew her closer still, the warmth of his body pervaded her: the aromatic scent of his after-shave and far more disturbing, the scent of the man himself. She couldn't concentrate on her dancing, and as he began kissing her she found herself responding with an abandon that made nonsense of any control she had hoped to exercise over her emotions.

For what seemed an eternity they clung together, kissing, touching, caressing, and her legs trembled beneath her.

'Darling,' he murmured. 'Darling, beautiful Leslie.'

Effortlessly he swung her off her feet, and as he carried her across the sitting-room to the bedroom, there was the soft whisper of silk as her négligé slipped to the floor. Gently he placed her on the bed and for a moment, eyes darkened by desire, he gazed down on her, drinking in her beauty.

Then swiftly he removed his robe and lay beside her, naked. Reaching out, he dimmed the lamp, and as rosy shadow blanked out reality, he gathered her close and explored every inch of her body with his mouth and tongue, arousing her to a raging fever of desire that enveloped them both in a world where time ceased to have any meaning.

Leslie's submission to Dane was total, her desire for

him as insatiable as his for her. Each time he took possession of her was more pleasurable than the last, for he was the most unselfish of lovers, always satisfying her before his own release.

The wonderful hunger that swept through them both made a mockery of her long-held belief that sex without love could hold no real satisfaction. Yet once or twice, in the far reaches of their passion-filled nights, she couldn't help but be riddled by guilt at the desire he aroused in her, and vowed to hold herself aloof from him; to submit to his demands but not respond. Yet he had only to touch her and her vow was forgotten. Nothing mattered but her need for him, and the exquisite feel of him inside her.

Their week in London flew by as they took in the sights by day and theatre and restaurants at night. Although she was no stranger to the town her knowledge of it was minimal compared with Dane's, and seeing it through his eyes she savoured it anew.

They hired a car and made several trips out of London, once to Windsor, ending the day with a never-to-be-forgotten dinner at the Waterside Inn. Situated on the Thames at Bray, it was justifiably as famous as its sister restaurant, Le Gavroche in London, where they had eaten several times.

Dane, true to his promise, brought Leslie a sable coat the first morning of their stay. They had not shopped since, and only on their last day did they decide to return to Knightsbridge. They window-shopped in Sloane Street, then headed for Harrods, the store that made the likes of Saks and Bergdorf Goodman pale into insignificance when it came to size, and variety of goods.

'I need some make-up,' Leslie said as they entered the Main Hall. 'Why don't you go up to China, and I'll join you as soon as I'm through?'

Nodding equably, Dane moved off. Among the items on the list for their house was a dinner-service they hoped to find here and ship back to Los Angeles.

Leslie watched his tall, broad frame disappear in the crowd before making her way to the Cosmetic Hall, stopping en route at the scarf counter to buy presents for her secretary and some close girl-friends.

Handing over her American Express card, she noticed a green cravat, the exact colour of the dress she was wearing. As she crossed to the other counter to examine it, she stopped in dismay. Charlene—whom she had last seen at Robert's funeral—was walking towards her! The shock was so great, Leslie was rooted to the spot. What foul luck to run across this bitch in a city of nine million people!

'Hullo, Charlene,' she said as the girl came abreast of her.

'Well, well, what a small world!' the redhead replied. 'Here on vacation?'

'On honeymoon, actually.'

Charlene's eyes riveted to the diamond eternity ring and huge marquise diamond engagement ring on Leslie's hand. 'Looks like you've done well for yourself,' she drawled. 'Who's the man?'

Did Charlene really not know, or was she feigning ignorance in the hope of embarrassing her?

'Dane Jordan,' Leslie stated.

'Dane!' Charlene almost shouted his name, making Leslie realise that her ignorance had been no pretence. 'I don't believe it!'

'Why not? You knew I was seeing him. The papers have been full of it for weeks.'

'Not the ones I've been reading. I've been in Italy for two months.'

So that's why I couldn't get hold of her, Leslie thought, for the day after agreeing to marry Dane, she had telephoned Charlene, worried in case the girl, learning of the engagement, called Dane and teased him about marrying her ex-stepdaughter—thus giving away Leslie's relationship with Robert.

Now, face to face with Charlene, she had the chance of trying out the bluff she had intended using at the time.

'I still thought you might have heard of my marriage from one of your friends,' she shrugged. 'By the way, Dane knows Robert was my stepfather.'

'I'm married too,' Charlene said, almost as though Leslie's remark was not worth commenting on. 'He's an Italian lawyer and we're living in Rome. I'm here on business with him, in fact.' Like a satisfied animal, she smoothed the fox coat she was wearing. And indeed there was something of the fox's slyness in her expression as she went on, 'So you married Dane. I must say you amaze me. Last time we spoke, you were furious with him for making me sell my shares to Imtex—and now you're his wife and sharing in the money he got from me! What a little schemer you are!'

'It takes one to know one,' Leslie said dulcetly, and retrieving her parcels and credit card from the salesgirl, turned on her heel and headed for the relative safety of the second floor.

'You were so long, I was beginning to think you'd bought the store!' grinned Dane as she found him in the Wedgwood section.

'Not quite.' Leslie had no intention of telling him why she had been delayed. 'Found something you like?'

'Yes—two services, both Rosenthal.'

"Let's go take a look, then.'

'Don't you want to browse around here first and see if there's anything else you prefer?'

'I trust your taste implicitly, darling. Let's pay and go.'

'A woman who wants to walk *out* of Harrods?' Dane said with mock incredulity. 'You must be the eighth wonder of the world!'

'Just a blushing bride who prefers to be alone with her husband,' Leslie cooed, clinging to his arm and praying she could get him out of the store before he bumped into Charlene.

Pulling him across to the Rosenthal section, she waited edgily as he debated which of the two services he wanted, and then discussed shipping arrangements. The talk seemed interminable and her nerve finally snapped.

'I must get some fresh air,' she gasped. 'I feel quite faint.'

With a hurried promise to call the salesman and finalise the remaining details, Dane propelled Leslie to the nearest lift, and once outside, hailed a cab to take them to the Mirabelle where he had booked a table.

'That's what comes from not having breakfast,' he reproved, slamming the cab door.

'I'll be fat as a house if I eat three meals a day,' Leslie protested. 'I think it's the sleepless nights that are exhausting me!'

'Complaining already?'

'Merely reminding you there are afternoons too!'

'What a great idea. Let's skip lunch and——'

'No!' she laughed. 'I'm faint from hunger, remember?'

'Then eat up quickly,' he said, and teasingly repeated the instruction some half-hour later as she cut into her *filet de boeuf* Lucullus, a house speciality.

'Are you always so impatient, Mr Jordan?' she smiled.

'Only when there's something I particularly want. And I always want *you*.'

'Shall I skip the sweet and coffee?'

'Would you be cross if I said yes?'

'I'd be cross if you didn't!'

His mouth moved sensuously, and beneath the table his hand lightly skimmed the top of her leg. 'That's what I love about you, Leslie. You want me as much as I want you, and you've no false modesty about showing it.'

His words made her hate herself for wanting a man she knew she should despise. Yet when she was in his arms she couldn't control her passion for him.

Not bothering with coffee, they returned to Claridges, and as the door of their suite closed behind them, he started to peel off her clothes. Like two eager children they clung together, exploring each other, neither of them able to hold back a moment longer. Then Dane slid inside her, plunging deep, ever deeper, filing her with his velvet hardness.

'Dearest angel heart,' he whispered against her throat, and gently began rotating his hips in a rhythm that became hers as she moved with him, and met him thrust for thrust, until their passion spiralled out of control as they came together in a wonderful, shuddering climax.

His body lay motionless on hers, his skin damp from exertion, and she pulled up the fine cotton sheet to cover him.

'Taking care of me, eh?' he murmured.

'I always take care of my investments!'

Laughter rumbled his chest, and raising his head he

looked down at her with a teasing smile.

'I'm glad we came back to the hotel.'

'Me too.' Leslie moved sinuously beneath him and his mouth curved with humour.

'Not yet, Mrs Joran,' he rolled off her. 'Superman I'm not!'

'You give a passable imitation!'

'Only because you're irresistible! Making love to you is a whole new experience for me.'

'Maybe what you feel for me is a new experience too?'

'Could be,' he mused. 'Stranger things have been known than husbands falling in love with their wives!'

It was impossible to tell if he meant it, or was merely trying to please her. But like his tender words during their lovemaking, she suspected it was little more than solace to her ego.

'When you've reached a conclusion, tell me.' She reached for her robe and slipped it on.

'Now you're angry.' Dane caught her arm and brought her down on the bed again.

'No, I'm not.' She remembered the part she was playing. 'It's just that I don't like being reminded of our one-sided relationship. This past week has been so perfect, I've tried to forget you only feel passion for me.'

Surprisingly, she meant what she said, and was deeply disturbed by it. It was dangerous to let herself soften towards him, though she realised this was the inevitable outcome of their lovemaking. After all, how could she think in terms of cold-blooded revenge after their shared intimacy? Which brought her to the sobering conclusion that the sooner she figured out how to get their marriage on to a platonic basis, the better.

'Don't knock the fact that we've a great sex life,' Dane said. 'That's the first step to a successful marriage. And believe me, ours can work as well as any other—even better perhaps, because we have to tread more warily with each other.'

'You may be right,' she answered, standing up again. 'But the real test won't start till we get back home.'

Home. At least she would be spared the final hypocrisy of sharing his new house with him, for it was still far from finished—and until it was, they'd be living in his apartment, the bachelor pad he had shared with countless other women, and where one more would make little if any imprint.

CHAPTER TEN

THEIR honeymoon slipped by all too quickly. Milan, apart from a visit to the Cathedral and La Scala, was little more than a shopping expedition, and neither of them was sorry to move on to Venice.

Despite the mid-November rain, it was an entrancing city, with a crystalline beauty all its own. Their hotel, the Gritti Palace on the Grand Canal, was only a short walk from the Piazza San Marco, surely the loveliest square in the world. Hand in hand they explored the cobbled streets and alleyways that led off it, and not even the mist and cold could keep them from a gondola ride on one of the waterways that crisscrossed the city like a cat's cradle.

Yet for all its haunting beauty, Leslie was left with an impression of sadness and decay; a city living on its past glory.

Paris, by contrast, was a city of today—despite its historical background—and it took her a while to adjust to the pace, so hard and fast after the slow, relaxing rhythm of Venice.

Her French was passable, but Dane's, surprisingly, was fluent, and when she commented on it, his reply was typical.

'What did you expect? It's the language of love, isn't it?'

Later, he told her he had worked there for a year as a travel courier before entering law school. He had returned frequently, and knew it like the back of his hand; which meant Leslie was shown a Paris far removed from the one she had visited a few years earlier. As in London, Dane had many friends here, and she liked them all. Well travelled, well heeled and sophisticated, they made it flatteringly plain that if she was good enough for Dane, she was good enough for them.

'Sorry to be leaving?' he asked, as they dined at Lasserre on their last night.

'Naturally. But all dreams come to an end—and I normally wake up to reality the moment I turn on the washing-machine!'

'My staff will take care of that in future,' he assured her. 'Just you concentrate on turning *me* on!'

Turning myself off, more like it, Leslie thought, as always far too aware of his magnetism. Another month alone with this man and she could end up putty in his hands; adoring him as all his girl-friends did!

'Why the frown?' he questioned.

'I was wondering how we'll behave towards each other once we're home and under pressure,' she lied.

'Same as we behave now. And we'll stand up OK to pressure too. Having someone to share your problems with, with whom you can relate and be honest, will do us both a helluva lot of good.'

'You sound as if you've given it quite a bit of thought.'

'I have. You've made me rethink a lot of things, my darling.'

He did not elaborate, and Leslie, wife of four weeks, knew him well enough not to probe.

Returning to Los Angeles, they were met at the airport by Dane's chauffeur, who drove them directly to the penthouse.

'Now isn't the time to carry you over the threshold,' Dane whispered in her ear as they stepped into the private elevator that led straight into the elegant entrance hall. 'I'll save that pleasure for our new home.'

'We'll be here at least another three months,' she warned.

'That's what comes of having a lousy architect!'

Laughing, she preceded him into the living-room, where the eclectic décor reflected her own taste.

Against a background of splendid proportions, the velvet-covered sofas, sycamore tables and modern pictures and sculptures took on a composition of elegant serenity. Sunshine tones suffused the whole apartment, and were reflected in lacquered walls of palest amber, floors of gold-veined white marble, and the fruit-drop colours of upholstery and curtains.

The living-room, dining-room and study were interlinked, and gave vistas of the city through french windows that led on to a flower-banked terrace. The main bedroom suite, with its massive bed, included a dressing-room and two bathrooms—on the off-chance that His and Hers weren't on speaking terms!

Leslie had dined in the apartment frequently when they were engaged, and did not feel a stranger here. Nor was she a stranger to the housekeeper and her husband, a Mexican couple who ran Dane's home and had gone out of their way to show how pleased they were that 'Mr D' had made such a sensible choice of wife.

'How kind of you, Conchita,' Leslie said gratefully, returning to the bedroom after a leisurely pre-dinner bath to find all her clothes neatly put away in the cupboards. 'But don't spoil me too much or you'll make me lazy.'

'I no theenk that happen,' the raven-haired woman said with a flash of white teeth. 'You very har' working lady and Pedro and I enjoy spoil you. If you unhappy with anything, and wan' done different, please no worry tell us.'

Over dinner, Leslie told Dane how welcoming Conchita had been, and he gave her a look of lazy amusement.

'She was always scared I'd settle on some starlet who'd lie in bed all day giving her orders! But with you she knows she has a mistress who'll leave her in charge!' He took a spoonful of gazpacho. 'We'll need more staff when we move house, though. It might be an idea to start looking around.'

'Let's wait till we're actually in,' Leslie suggested. 'Then Conchita will have a better idea of how many we need.'

'Good thinking. I'm glad you're not just a beautiful face!' He leered at her. 'By the way, I'm opening an account for you at my bank. I'd like you to come with me tomorrow to sign the necessary papers.'

'I don't need an account,' she said quickly. 'I have my own money.'

'I know. But I'll get a kick out of knowing you're spending mine. It'll do my libido good to see you in a black lace bra and frontless panties that I know I've paid for!'

Leslie fluttered her lashes at him, resisting the urge to box his ears. Frontless panties indeed! An iron chastity belt if she had her way. But not yet. First things first. And the first was to be a doting wife for a few months. But after that . . . She hugged the thought to herself.

'I'll get you charge accounts at the top stores too,' Dane went on. 'Leave me a list of where you like to shop and my secretary will see to it.'

'Aren't you afraid I'll be too extravagant?' Leslie asked.

'Not in the least. You're so careful with the costs of our new home, it's my least worry.'

It will be your greatest before I've finished with you, she vowed, and itched to put her plans into action.

Just then Pedro came in with a stuffed crown roast of lamb, and they waited silently while he served them.

'I think I'll turn in early and take a sleeping-pill,' Leslie went on when they were alone again. 'I'll need a clear head in the morning, when I tackle four weeks' backlog!'

'I doubt I can get to sleep so early,' Dane grunted. 'I'm tired, but restless.'

'Take a sleeping-pill.'

'Maybe I will.' He sipped his wine. 'Jet-lag is the one thing that makes me dislike air travel.'

'Well, we aren't likely to be going on any long journeys for a while, are we?'

'Not unless you count Philadelphia.' He caught her puzzled look. 'We'll be spending Christmas there with my family.'

'I wish you'd told me before,' Leslie said. 'Marybeth and Jack asked us to stay with them in San Francisco, and I accepted.'

'Seems we'll offend someone whatever we do,' Dane sighed. 'It might be more diplomatic if we spend it on our own.'

It was not a statement with which Leslie could argue.

'What say we go to Hawaii?' he went on. 'You've never been there, and the Mauna Lani Bay Hotel is the best in the Pacific.'

'Sounds fabulous,' she said.

In all honesty she hadn't relished being with her cousins over Christmas, for by then—if things panned out as she hoped—she would be starting to make Dane's life a misery, and her marriage would have a sour edge to it that was bound to provoke questions from Marybeth.

'Will we get a booking with Christmas only a month away?' she went on.

'I'll pull a few strings,' he said confidently. 'The manager's a friend of a friend.'

There were no problems with their families or the resort, where Dane managed to secure a suite for a week, though Leslie, overhearing the conversation, knew the booking was very much in the nature of a favour.

'We've dozens of invitations to New Year parties,' he stated, settling beside her on the settee. 'Would you like to go through them and decide which you'd like to accept?'

'They're *your* friends, so it's best if you decide,' Leslie said docilely.

'OK,' he agreed, looking pleased. 'But in future, our social arrangements are your responsibility. For the next twenty-five years, though, I prefer having you to myself!' He drew her close. 'Let's go to bed, darling, I haven't made love to you in over a day!'

'If you hire a private jet next time we go on a long journey, you can overcome that problem!' she smiled.

Leaving Dane to switch off the lights, she went into the bedroom. She hadn't yet taken off her dress when he came up behind her and unzipped it, pulling her down on the bed and taking her with a swift fierceness that left her gasping. But as always he was tender afterwards, cradling her close and murmuring endearments. Gradually she felt his arousal again, and as he went to slide her beneath him, she wriggled free.

'We've got to take our sleeping-pills,' she reminded him.

'Must we?' he said huskily. 'Trouble is they'll make us sleep through the night, and it seems such a waste!'

'There's always the morning,' she murmured softly. 'You don't have far to go to the office.'

'True.' He gave a contented sigh and snuggled into the pillows.

'I'll get your pill,' Leslie said, touching her hand to his cheek as she slipped out of bed.

In the bathroom she took a tablet from the bottle, and filled a glass with water.

'Here you are, sweetheart,' she said, coming back with it.

'Had yours?' he asked as he swallowed it.

'I took it in the bathroom,' she lied. Plan one was about to be set in motion.

Within minutes, Dane's even breathing told her he was asleep. But Leslie waited an hour before attempting to wake him. She had read somewhere that drugged sleep was the deepest sleep of all, and difficult to return to once broken.

'Darling,' she called, digging him in the ribs. He stayed dead to the world, and she nudged him again, harder this time.

'Wha—whasa matter?' His lids lifted a slit.

'You're snoring,' she said plaintively, 'and you woke me up.'

'Sorry, dar . . .' He turned on to his back.

A few seconds later, what she had read went out of the window, for he was out for the count again! Impatiently she glared at the luminous dial of the bedside clock, then after the longest half-hour she could recollect spending, she shook him hard again.

He jack-knifed into a sitting position and looked at her dazedly.

'You're still snoring,' she said in a small voice.

'Forgive me,' he mumbled, his mind clearly fuzzy. 'Maybe if I sleep on my side . . .'

Leslie watched as he made himself comfortable, only the top of his gleaming black head visible showing above the terracotta silk sheets. This time she let an hour tick away.

Then: 'Dane! *Wake up!*' Her only answer was a faint grunt and she prodded his shoulder viciously. 'Dane, you're snoring like a pneumatic drill and I can't get to sleep!'

With a deep sigh, he turned on to his other side. Once more silence reigned, and she knew he was in the land of Nod. How lucky men were to fall asleep so easily. Not that Dane's luck was going to last. She would give him another half-hour and start again. She yawned, wishing there was a way of exhausting him without exhausting herself! Still, she had started this and intended finishing it.

The minutes ticked by, slow as a lame tortoise. But at last the little hand reached three and the large one twelve, and she drew a deep breath and bellowed, '*Dane!*'

Instantly he jerked awake. 'What is it? You ill?'

'I've got a splitting headache. Your snoring's kept me awake all night.'

Dazedly he shifted round to face her. 'I'm sorry, sweetheart. It's the first time I've been told I snore.'

'Wives can afford to be more truthful than girl-friends!'

'But we've been sleeping together for a month!'

'Not in L.A.,' she said quickly. 'Maybe it's something to do with the smog.'

'Then there isn't much we can do about it. We can't move to another city, so you'll have to grin and bear it.'

'I can't,' she complained. 'I'll be a nervous wreck in a week. I'm sure I read recently of some new kind of operation they do.'

'*Operation*?' Dane was fully alert now, and he switched on the bedside lamp. 'No one's going to mess around with *my* nose!' He touched it, as if to reassure himself it was still there. 'It may not be perfect, but it's been a good friend for thirty-five years!'

'Surgery won't do anything to the shape, darling,' she assured him. 'Nor will it harm your sense of taste and smell. They say that sort of thing only happens in five per cent of cases.'

'Five per cent!' He was aghast. 'That's a damned high percentage.'

Trying to keep a straight face, Leslie watched him through her lashes, aware that mention of the word 'surgery' and the high failure rate would keep him miles away from a doctor's consulting room.

'You're very knowledgeable on the subject,' he muttered.

'Only because the husband of one of my girl-friends snores non-stop.'

'He obviously didn't have this operation, then!'

'No. Their doctor didn't agree with it and advised separate bedrooms.'

Dane pulled a face. 'Sounds like an equally painful cure!'

'We can always part,' Leslie said with a little-girl laugh as she snuggled up to him. 'I read somewhere that snoring can be grounds for divorce.'

'Try it, and I'll get every one of my exes to testify in my defence!'

'I'd get a tape recorder and prove them liars!'

'OK, you've talked me out of that one.' His mouth twitched humorously. 'How about a peg on my nose?'

Leslie had to smile at the image it conjured up. 'Effective perhaps, but hardly conducive to romance.'

'Don't sneer before you've seen it. Lady Hamilton found Lord Nelson's eye-patch irresistible!' Dane's hand slid underneath Leslie's nightgown. 'Speaking of romance, how about indulging in some ourselves now our sleep's been ruined anyway?'

Leslie forced a yawn and gave him a gentle push. 'There's four hours to go before our alarm call, and that's better than nothing. I'm exhausted and I'm going to try out the dressing-room. I only hope I won't hear your snores from there.'

'*I'll* go,' Dane said gallantly. 'But don't expect me to be like your friend's husband. I'm old-fashioned where marriage is concerned, and don't approve of separate rooms.'

'You don't have to preach to the converted,' she replied, and leaning across the bed, kissed him lightly on the lips.

But despite Dane's assertion, by the end of two weeks, sheer exhaustion drove him into the dressing-room permanently, for Leslie had relentlessly woken him three or four times night after night. Separate rooms might not diminish his sexual need of her, but it would undoubtedly lessen the togetherness that came from sharing a bed, where he would cradle her close and unburden himself of all the problems of the day, as she in turn had found herself doing with him. Indeed it had been surprisingly comforting to have a broad, protective shoulder to lean on, and an intelligent mind that pierced through the gloom of her worries and made them less onerous.

His understanding and compassion surprised her,

making his toughness in court all the harder to comprehend, and she analysed it continuously, unable to work out why he didn't focus his talents on something constructive rather than destructive.

She was certain it had nothing to do with the financial rewards from this side of the law. Dane was brilliant enough to make his name in any branch. Nor was it because it gave him entry into the world of glitter and glamour that might otherwise have been shut to him, for since his marriage he seemed as happy to stay home alone with her as to go out.

So why was he so ruthless professionally? As always the answer eluded her, and though intuition told her his scathing denunciation of December/May marriages stemmed from a personal reason, she knew he would never admit it to any woman—particularly one he had married because it was the only way of getting her into his bed!

CHAPTER ELEVEN

THE weeks leading to Christmas flew by, and basking in the aura of a husband who was happy to indulge her every whim, Leslie frequently had to remind herself that she had married Dane to make him suffer—not be happy!

Despite separate rooms, their physical relationship had not diminished one jot. While it had lost some of its spontaneity, this was more than compensated for by its frequency. It was as if Dane could not have enough of her, and she in turn found herself attracted to him like a moth to a flame.

He had only to look at her, touch her, to set her alight. It was a response that she felt demeaned her, turned her into a primeval being with no control over her emotions, and she became increasingly afraid of being trapped in a sexual abyss from which there would be no escape. After all, how could one cold-bloodedly plot the downfall by day of a man with whom you shared the greatest intimacy by night?

Which brought her to the loaded question. How to stop his lovemaking yet have him believe the abstinence was hurting her as much as him?

Her reason would have to be watertight, and the only acceptable one was to feign illness. A slipped disc perhaps? But that would mean acting the invalid, and she had no intention of staying away from the office. A broken leg? That was out for the same reason, and she restlessly paced her room, unable to concentrate on the plans she was drawing up for a school in West Hollywood.

Marriage to Dane was occupying too much of her thoughts, not only because she was busy devising and discarding schemes that would eventually lead them into the divorce court, but because she was desperately trying to hold her emotions aloof from their life together, a task she was finding increasingly difficult.

For this reason alone their sexual intimacy had to be nipped in the bud, not that 'bud' was the right word. Full-grown passion flower more like it! Momentarily she closed her eyes, remembering this past weekend. Conchita and Pedro had gone away for two nights, and she and Dane had decided to stay at home and catch up on some work. To this end, he had switched on the answering machine and drawn the curtains in case any friends took it into their heads to drop by.

None had, but nor had any work been done. The simple casserole Leslie had elected to make as a change from Conchita's more elaborate cooking had gone down so well that Dane had insisted on helping her tidy the kitchen. The sight of him in an apron had made her laugh so much that he had chased her round the living-room to extort a penance.

Not surprisingly the penance was paid for on the roomy settee, and led to the abandonment of all further work for the evening. Saturday passed the same way, both of them in lounging pyjamas, munching ad-hoc meals as and when the fancy took them, though their main fancy was directed towards possessing each other.

'This can't go on,' Leslie muttered to herself. 'I *must* stop him making love to me.'

The very word 'love' made her hackles rise, reminding her that as far as Dane was concerned she was simply a sex object he wanted to possess.

'I've got to think of an illness,' she said again, speaking aloud in the hope that it might help her find one. It daren't be too specific because that could lead to problems, so why not say it was gynaecological, and leave it at that? It covered a multitude of ailments, and was an area most men found embarrassing to discuss. If Dane didn't prove to be one of them, he was bound to respect *her* reticence, and attribute it to newly-wed reserve.

Determined not to waste time, she told her secretary she wasn't feeling well, and left the office early, repeating the same lie to Conchita on reaching the apartment, where she put herself to bed to emphasise the point.

Fetchingly attired in baby-pink lace, with matching satin ribbon confining her gold-blonde hair, Leslie proceeded to study the medical tome she had collected from the library on her way home. With her face devoid of make-up, save a touch of mascara on her long lashes, she looked young and innocent as she nestled against the frilly white satin pillows.

By the time she heard Dane's incisive step, she knew more than she wanted to know about the female anatomy. Most of the book had been too technical for a layman, but she had nevertheless absorbed sufficient jargon to impress anyone but a doctor.

Feigning sleep, she waited till Dane was beside the bed before slowly opening her eyes. How handsome he was, towering above her, his expression tender, his dark eyes filled with a concern she found both surprising and confusing.

'Why—why are you home so early?' she asked sleepily.

'It's not early, darling—it's past seven.'

'Impossible!' she gasped. 'You mean I've been asleep three hours?'

'You have.' He seated himself on the bed beside her. 'Conchita says you aren't well.'

'I keep getting pains in my stomach.'

'Have you spoken to the doctor?'

'No. It's probably something I ate for lunch. I'm sure I'll be fine in the morning.'

'If you're not, I'll take you to see him.'

She yawned prettily. 'I'm afraid I haven't called the Barbers to say I don't feel up to having dinner with them, but there's no reason why you can't go without me.'

'I wouldn't dream of leaving you.' Dane slid an arm beneath her back and pressed his mouth tenderly to her shoulder. 'I'll go and phone them, then get Conchita to serve us something on a tray.'

Nothing Leslie said could dissuade him from remaining by her side, and after their meal he donned his dressing-gown and watched television with her, then insisted on staying until she fell asleep.

Waking at seven next morning, she was astonished to find Dane out for the count in the armchair beside her bed. He had clearly spent the night there. Stubble darkened the line of his jaw, softening its aggressiveness, and lending him a look of vulnerability that gave her an unwelcome urge to smooth away the lines either side of his mouth.

As if aware of being watched, his eyes flew open, and he stretched lazily, giving her a tired but warm smile. 'How do you feel, my darling?'

'Well enough to go to the office. But you shouldn't have stayed with me. I told you there was nothing much wrong.'

'At least my snoring didn't disturb you.' He paused. 'Or did it?'

'Only as far as waking me this morning,' she lied.

'I was worried you'd feel ill in the night, and I wouldn't hear you call me. You know what a heavy sleeper I am.' He shrugged broad shoulders.

'You don't look as if you got much sleep last night,' she said. 'Why didn't you come and lie on the bed?'

'I was less likely to snore sitting up!' He yawned again. 'One restless night won't harm me. Before moving into the dressing-room I had fourteen in a row!'

Leslie stifled a laugh, and watched him saunter to the door. 'I'll go shower and shave. Do you feel up to having breakfast with me?'

Leslie nodded, realising she was ravenous. Hardly surprising, considering she had made herself refuse supper last night!

'I think I can manage a little something,' she said carefully.

'Good. See you in twenty minutes, then.'

That evening Dane returned home to find her in bed again, though to forestall him calling her doctor, she told him she had seen one on her way home.

'He's arranged for me to see a gynaecologist in the morning,' she elaborated. 'He thinks it's some kind of infection.'

'I'm going with you,' Dane stated.

'You can't. You have to be in court. Anyway, there's no need. I'm not having an operation—only an examination!'

'OK. But call my secretary as soon as you're out, and she'll get a message to me.'

Leslie could not help being touched by his solicitude, but reminded herself he deserved everything he was getting.

Next day he was home by five, and Leslie, coming out of the shower, bumped into him as he walked into the bathroom.

'Hey!' he smiled, steadying her in his arms. 'I could have given you a black eye.'

How easy it would be to pretend it wasn't accidental, she mused, storing away yet another snippet for her war of attrition.

'My mind was miles away, darling,' she smiled back. 'How come you're home this early?'

'I was worried about you and wanted to be sure I'd got your message right. So everything's OK, is it?'

'Sort of.' Leslie knotted the sash of her towelling robe more securely around her slender waist, and perched on the edge of the bed. The slightly damp material clung to her body, outlining her firm breasts, the skirt parting to reveal long, shapely legs. Poor Dane, she thought, seeing him eye them hungrily. For all the pleasure he'd be getting from them, they might well be made of wood!

'My doctor was right,' she continued. 'I have an infection and have to be on antibiotics for a few months.'

'Are you sure it's nothing serious?' Dane asked anxiously.

'Yes, but . . .' Leslie lowered her head and looked away from him, giving every sign of being nervous.

'But what?' Taking her chin with a firm but gentle hand, he turned it his way. 'Out with it, Leslie, I'm your husband and I want the truth.'

Still refusing to meet his gaze—there was no way he could control her eyeballs!—she stammered, 'It's d-definitely not serious, but the gynaecologist s-said I—

said we shouldn't make love till it's cleared up completely.'

'Is that all?' The tightness in Dane's voice had disappeared completely, and glancing quickly at his face, she saw his smile was broad. 'For a minute you had me running scared!'

'Scared?'

'I've grown used to having you around, and I ...' His smile vanished, leaving him sober and older looking as he put his arm around her waist and drew her back to rest against him. 'Sex is an important part of our relationship, sweetheart, but these past months have shown me that a good marriage has much more going for it than that.' He placed his cheek upon hers and breathed in the fragrance of her. 'And that's what we have, Leslie, a real good marriage. I've never been happier in my life.'

'You sound like a man in love,' she teased.

He released her with startling abruptness. 'Isn't it enough for you that I'm happy with you? Must you nag for the stars as well as the moon?'

The words stung her to anger, yet unaccountably also brought her to the verge of tears. But not until she was alone again—Dane having gone to change—did she try to work out why he consistently managed to arouse such mixed emotions in her; one minute making her melt in his arms, the next, whipping her into such fury that vengeance for her stepfather's death seemed the only path to pursue. The trouble was, she couldn't sustain either feeling for long, and she felt as if she were perched on a seesaw—up one moment, down the next.

In the ensuing weeks her emotions continued to vacillate. Believing her to be below par healthwise, Dane insisted on curtailing their social life, which meant they spent many evenings and most weekends alone together. Yet they were never bored with each other's company, and found innumerable things to discuss and do together: driving out of town to explore the countryside, browsing in bookshops and poking assiduously in junk yards.

'Soon as we're in our new home,' he pronounced one Sunday, 'I'm going to turn one of the rooms into a painting studio.'

'I never knew you were a painter.'

'Watercolour's always been a hobby of mine.'

This surprised her even more, for when he had mentioned painting, she had envisaged him in front of an outsize canvas, sloshing on colours with a large brush. Yet thinking about it, she could see him being an excellent watercolourist, for he was a stickler for detail, and was extremely neat and tidy.

'What's *your* hobby?' he broke into her thoughts.

'Knitting,' she confessed.

He stared at her, then collapsed with laughter. 'Knitting? You're having me on!'

'What's funny about knitting?'

'Nothing. And my mother's the world's best. But it's not something I ever associated with a five-foot-eight curvaceous blonde!'

'Shows how stereotyped your mind is,' sniffed Leslie. 'I happen to be pretty damn good at it.'

'Then I'd like a sweater for my birthday,' he said promptly. 'Navy or grey, in fine cashmere.'

'All you'll get from me is chunky knit. I like quick results!'

She waited for him to make some sexy comment, but he didn't. Come to think of it, since their life of celibacy he had avoided all talk of sex, apart from one evening when they had petted so heavily that she had found herself but a moment away from orgasm.

Subsequently she had told him—with a great deal of pseudo embarrassment—that her gynaecologist had advised her to steer clear of any kind of arousal, and Dane had accepted the injunction without argument and had sought other ways of keeping them both occupied. She was not surprised therefore when, learning of her interest in knitting, he returned home on the Monday following their conversation with a pattern for a sweater and some black and white flecked wool, together with several painting manuals for himself.

Their cosy evenings together continued, and Leslie increasingly wondered if she had been wise to fake illness, for being alone with him was putting a great strain on her. It appeared to have the opposite effect on Dane, who had never looked happier.

For the first time in years she found herself dreading Christmas, afraid that once they were alone in Hawaii, he would lose his self-control and persuade her—which would be all too easy—to lose hers.

But here too he proved her wrong, for despite the romantic setting, his platonic behaviour never wavered. Leslie was discomfited by the strength of her own sexual drive, and one morning as they sunbathed on the terrace outside their suite it was all she could do not to reach out to him.

Dane, oblivious of her erotic thoughts, acted like a loving brother. They swam, snorkelled, went canal paddling, golfed, played tennis, and then revived themselves on sunbeds on the palm-shaded beach. Without doubt the Mauna Lani lived up to its name, for translated it meant 'mountain reaching to heaven'.

'We'll come back in the spring,' Dane promised as their plane bore them high above Waikiki and

Diamond Head, en route for Los Angeles. 'It's just the place to make babies!'

Leslie bit her lip. So what if Dane was happily planning a family! This time next year their marriage would be over, and he would probably be winging his way across the emerald ocean with another sex object.

As always, the thought of him with another woman filled her with anger, and she was dismayed by her dog-in-the-manger attitude. She didn't want Dane herself, yet she hated the idea of anyone else having him!

Her depression intensified when, early in January, he went to New York on business for a week. Left alone for the first time since their marriage, she was devastated at how dependent she had become on him as companion and friend, and though she was asked out every night for dinner, without him there was no enjoyment, merely a marking time until his return.

'I think we're due to give a party,' he announced over breakfast, a few days afterwards. 'Our house won't be ready for months, and we owe so many people—if you're up to coping with it, that is? I don't want to put a strain on you.'

Guiltily Leslie shook her head. 'I'm fine, dear. You fuss over me too much.'

'I enjoy fussing over you.' He hesitated. 'When are you seeing the speialist again?'

'I see him regularly for check-ups, but I'm afraid we still can't——'

'That wasn't why I was asking,' he intervened. 'I'm not putting any pressure on you, sweetheart. I just want to know if you're getting better.'

'I'm doing fine,' she asserted, and quickly returned to the subject of the party. 'Give me a list of who you want to invite and I'll call them.'

Dane glanced at his watch and hastily downed his coffee. 'I must run, darling. I'm meeting the District Attorney at eight-thirty.'

'Don't tell me *he's* getting divorced?'

Dane shook his head, but vouchsafed nothing further. 'I'll let you have the list this evening.'

He brought it home with him, and the next day Leslie set about the arrangements.

'I forgot to ask if it's formal,' he questioned as the day of the party drew nearer.

'Informal,' she said. 'I'm sorry I didn't think to ask you.'

'No matter. You're the boss in household affairs!'

But what about affairs outside the house? she thought, and wondered if he was indulging in any. If he were, it would account for his easy acceptance of their celibate marriage. Yet when did he find time to see someone else? He worked like a demon by day, and was with her each night. No, much as she would like to see him as a roué, she had to give the devil his due and admit he was behaving exemplarily. Of course she had caught him looking at her on occasion like a hungry shark, but never by word or gesture had he said anything to make her feel guilty or unhappy.

'You will, won't you?'

Startled out of her reverie, she looked at him blankly.

'I asked if you were going to buy yourself a new dress for the party,' he repeated.

'I don't think so. If it's informal there's no need.'

'There's every need,' he said drily. 'Your idea of "informal" is trousers, but my friends would see it as wearing their second-best diamonds!'

'I take it you want me to splash out on a fancy little number, then?'

'The fancier the better. Why not try that new boutique on Rodeo Drive? I've heard they have a fantastic selection.'

'How come you're so knowledgeable?' she asked sweetly.

'Jane Barret was talking about it.' He named the latest divorcee he was acting for. 'She's just bought herself a whole new wardrobe there.'

'With the outrageous settlement you got her, I'm surprised she didn't buy the shop!'

'She's thinking about it,' he chuckled.

'Don't you have any conscience?' Leslie snapped. 'She was only married five years and you got her a million for everyone of them.'

'But think what her husband got!' Dane gave an exaggerated leer, and Leslie controlled her temper.

'Anyway, try that boutique,' he repeated. 'You might find something you like.'

'As they only stock Valentinos, Ungaros and Lagerfelds, I'm bound to. I hope you realise how much they cost?'

'I can afford it, sweetheart. Buy whatever takes your fancy.'

His answer played directly into her hands.

Taking 'whatever takes your fancy' literally, Leslie went to the boutique later that morning. Their clothes were stunning, and she found it impossible to decide between the four outfits they showed her. But then why bother with anything as mundane as a decision when Dane could afford the lot?

Airily she bought them all, but hearing the total cost, almost changed her mind, almost, but not quite. After all, she was only carrying out her master plan. With a flourish she wrote out a cheque amd went on her merry way, rushing from store to store and spending money like water.

Dane was not forgotten either. It would have been selfish to spend his money entirely on herself! And though she entered the Porsche showroom with some misgivings, they disappeared the instant she seated herself behind the wheel of their newest and most expensive model. A short spin around the block decided her, and she bought it and asked for it to be delivered at eight o'clock that evening.

The salesman showed no surprise, for this was after all movieland, where affluence had reached its apotheosis, and forty-thousand-dollar cars were snapped up quicker than four-thousand-dollar ones.

The Porsche was her last purchase, and she made her way home on a high, her adrenalin stimulated by this final act of profligacy. Triumphantly she recalled Dane's interpretation of her stepfather's cancellation of Charlene's credit cards as the action of a Scrooge, rather than that of a husband worried by his wife's orgy of extravagance. Well, now she was giving Dane a taste of his own medicine!

'Had a good day, darling?' he asked as he walked through the door later that evening.

'Wonderful,' she enthused. 'Though whether you'll agree with me is another matter.' Taking his hand, she led him into the bedroom.

A lesser man might have blanched at sight of the clothes piled on the bed, and the boxes, bags and shoes strewn higgledy-piggledy over the floor. Deliberately Leslie hadn't tidied up, deciding the impact would be far more devastating this way. But to her astonishment Dane appeared unperturbed and merely gave her bottom an affectionate pat.

'Aiming to make the best-dressed woman's list at one go?' he smiled.

'I hope you don't think I've been too extravagant?' Leslie said in a little-girl voice. 'But you did say I could get anything I want, so I did. And more to *your* taste.' Cunningly she placed the onus on him.

'I like the way you dress,' he protested.

'But you think it's a bit understated, don't you?'

'Let's just say that with your looks and figure I think you can afford to be more dramatic.'

'Tell me if this is dramatic enough,' Leslie said, and rummaging among the pile for an Ungaro, went swiftly into the bathroom to put it on.

Emerging, she struck a model girl's pose. 'Like it?'

Dane's astonished silence was answer enough as he gawped at the frou-frou concoction of black lace over turquoise silk, sashed just below the hip, and flounced to well above the knee. The bodice was minimal, sustained only by two narrow straps.

'You won't fade into the background wearing that!' he told her.

'You sound as if you don't like it?'

'On the contrary. It's stunning and you look gorgeous.'

Leslie gave an audible sigh of relief. 'For a moment I had visions of returning it.' She took a pile of bills from her handbag and handed them to him. 'Do you want to look through these before dinner?'

'I'll reserve my indigestion for afterwards! And take that worried look of your face. I'm delighted you've bought yourself a few things.'

So this was what he called a few things! Well, she would see if she could do better next time. 'Wait till you see what I bought *you*,' she said. 'You might change your mind!'

'I doubt it. I enjoy receiving gifts—even when I'm paying for them! I'll close my eyes so you can surprise me,' he said good-naturedly.

Leslie suppressed a giggle as she pictured his face when he saw the scarlet Porsche.

A knock at the door interrupted them, and Pedro came in to say a Mr Bonner was waiting downstairs to see her.

'Tell him we'll be down in five minutes.' Leslie pretended not to notice Dane's puzzled expression and went back into the bathroom.

'Who is this guy?' he called after her.

'No one special.'

'Then why are we going downstairs to see him?'

'Because there's no need for him to come up.'

'You must have a diploma in evasion,' Dane muttered as she reappeared.

'Coming from a lawyer, I take that as a compliment!'

'I hate mysteries,' he grumbled as they stepped into the elevator and she pressed the garage button. 'What's it all about?'

'Stop being an old grouse and relax. I've told you it's a surprise.'

But the surprise was Leslie's. Expecting Dane to show anger—at the very least shock—he disappointed her by being delighted.

'What a beauty!' He ran a hand along the sleek bonnet. 'I couldn't have bought myself anything better!'

'And you don't think it's too expensive?'

'It's cheaper than a Rolls!' He patted the bonnet again. 'We'll take her for a run after dinner,' he said as the salesman left. 'We could go to the Polo Lounge for a drink.'

'You just want to show off the car,' Leslie smiled, amused by the touch of the small boy in even Dane.

'And my beautiful wife too,' he added, and putting an arm affectionately round her waist, walked with her back to the elevator.

CHAPTER TWELVE

LESLIE decided to wait until after the party before considering any further ways of annoying Dane. She had to admit she was finding it increasingly easy to put off till tomorrow what she should have done yesterday, and had actually reached the point of asking herself whether it might not be better to forget the past and try to build a real future with him.

There was no denying she had found a certain happiness with him. And sexual pleasure too, for she wanted him so much, it was all she could do to carry on with her pretended ill-health!

Often, when they were alone, she felt herself on the verge of confessing everything, only to be held back by the fear that if he learned the real reason she had married him, it would kill stone-dead any feelings he might have for her.

Yet what exactly were his feelings? He was still master of his tongue, and even at the height of his desire, the word 'love' never passed his lips, which went to prove that whatever else she might think of him, she could never accuse him of being a liar!

But though he didn't love her, he enjoyed hearing her say how much *she* loved him. And the more she professed it, the happier he was, basking in her affection like a cat in front of a fire. Slowly but surely she had noticed a change in him: a greater desire to be alone with her, which reaffirmed her belief that when she finally walked out on him, his ego would suffer a terrible blow.

But that lay ahead. For the moment she would remain the loving wife.

The party they gave was an enormous success, and no one seeing Leslie play the ecstatically happy hostess would have guessed at the turmoil raging within her.

She had taken extra pains with her appearance, and was relieved to find how make-up could transform a drawn face into a vibrant one. Her dress helped too, and the admiring glances of Dane's friends told her she had made the right choice. The clinging turquoise and black silk showed off her body to perfection, while the eye-catching length, exposing her shapely legs encased in sheer black tights, made her appear even taller than she was.

'I guess your next party will be in your new house,' Beverly commented when dinner was over and the staff were clearing the centre of the room for dancing. She and Leslie had struck up a good friendship and lunched together once a week. 'I drove by it yesterday and went in and nosed around. Hope you don't mind?'

'Why should I?' Leslie smiled. 'I've already told you you're welcome to.'

'Am I interrupting anything?'

It was Caldwell, come to claim his wife for a rumba, and a few seconds later Leslie found herself in the arms of Hal Dawson, Dane's close friend and accountant. Tall, and well-built, he was good-looking in a laid-back way, with fair skin, light grey eyes and sleek blond hair. He had been at college with Dane, and their careers had followed equally successful paths.

'I hear you're off to La Costa tomorrow,' he said conversationally, as they moved around the floor.

'Yes. I'm meeting my cousins there. I'm building a

house for them nearby, and they're spending a week at the Spa. I'm only sorry Dane's too busy to come with me.'

'So am I. He drives himself too hard. You should get him to slow down.'

'He loves his work.'

'He loves you more, and he'd listen to you.'

'If that were true he'd stop handling divorce!'

'Given his background,' Hal said, 'I can see why he enjoys it.'

'What's his background to do with it?'

Hal stumbled, and apologised profusely, explaining he danced so rarely that he was rusty. But Leslie knew it was her question, rather than his ineptitude, that had made him clumsy.

'Don't pretend with me, Hal. Just tell me why Dane's background has affected his career.'

'Well, it's—er——' Hal stopped, clearly uncomfortable. 'Heck! I wish I'd kept my mouth shut.'

'But you didn't and you can't backtrack now.'

'I just took it for granted Dane had told you about his father,' Hal muttered, still reluctant to come clean.

'All he said was his father died years ago.'

'He hates talking about it,' Hal conceded. 'I only learned the story myself the night we graduated, when Dane had drunk too much. But I'm surprised he hasn't told *you*.'

Because he doesn't love me, Leslie thought, and was inexplicably saddened that Dane should have kept secret something which, according to his closest friend, had affected his life.

'Come on, Hal, quit stalling,' she said sensing he would be more forthcoming if she played it lightly.

'I'd rather let Dane tell you.'

So much for the lightness act! Leslie could

cheerfully have shaken him.

'OK,' she shrugged. 'Have it your way, But it might have helped me understand him better. He's still quite a mystery to me.'

Hal went on dancing in silence, his expression indicative of a desire to answer her question, but a reluctance to break his friend's confidence.

'Let's go on to the terrace,' he pronounced unexpectedly, and steered her outside to a red and white striped hammock at the far end.

Even after they had settled themselves on the gently swinging seat he said nothing, and Leslie had almost decided he wasn't going to when he spoke.

'Dane's father walked out on his wife and family for someone young enough to be his daughter. And this apparently after fifteen years' wedded bliss—or so his had wife thought.

'I see.' And Leslie did. Saw so much more than she had bargained for, and got a totally new slant on Dane's character. But there was more to come, and as she heard it, she was stunned.

'As if walking out on his wife and young children wasn't bad enough,' Hal continued, 'the bastard actually sold his business, took out a huge mortgage on his home, cleaned out their joint bank account, and disappeared into the blue beyond, so Mrs Jordan couldn't even sue for maintenance! It wasn't until years later—when he was killed in a car crash—that she found out he'd been living in Arizona.'

'What a dreadful story! You read about things like that, yet never imagine them happening to people you know. But why didn't Mrs Jordan hire a private detective to look for him?'

'She couldn't afford to! Every cent she had went on keeping the girls at college, and Dane at school. With the help of her bank manager she opened a dry-cleaning store, and only sold it when her daughters were married and Dane had established his career. The rest you know.'

Leslie nodded. Easy to understand now why Dane always represented the wife in a divorce case; why he showed no mercy for the man. He obviously associated every female client with his deserted mother, and their husband with the father who had to be made to pay for abandoning his wife and children. The hurt boy had become the hurt man, and because he had seen how 'love' had destroyed his father's integrity, he had determined never to marry or be controlled by love himself.

Thoughtfully Leslie rubbed the wedding ring on her finger. Yet despite his feelings, Dane *had* capitulated to marriage, and who was to say he wouldn't eventually succumb to love too?

'I hope you won't let on that I've told you all this?' Hal said nervously, 'I'm sure Dane will eventually tell you.'

'I won't breathe a word,' Leslie promised. 'Anyway, his mother's coming to stay with us at the end of the month, so he's sure to mention something before she arrives.'

'If he doesn't, I bet Mrs Jordan will. She's a disarmingly honest and charming woman. An ideal mother-in-law.'

'You should know!' 'Leslie couldn't resist saying, for Hal was in the process of unhitching himself for the third time.

'For my next marriage,' he retorted, rising and pulling her up with him, 'I intend finding myself an orphan!'

Laughing, they returned to the dance-floor.

It was two o'clock before the party broke up, and with the departure of the last guest, Leslie heaved an audible sigh of relief.

'Glad it's over?' asked Dane as she flopped into an armchair and kicked off her black silk pumps.

'Glad to get out of these.' She massaged her toes. 'They're sitting shoes, not dancing ones!'

'Beats me why women torture themselves in the name of fashion. You should have worn flat heels.'

'They wouldn't go with the dress!'

'Anything would go with that dress. You were the belle of the ball.'

'Thank you, kind sir,' she smiled.

'Hal seemed to think so too.' Dane's voice was casual, though the deep brown eyes were probing. 'He paid you a helluva lot of attention.'

'Stop playing the jealous husband,' she reproved. 'He's your best friend!'

'Then what was my best friend saying to you on the terrace? Confiding the story of his life?'

Leslie nearly blurted out 'No, yours,' but remembering her promise to Hal, stopped herself.

'His marriages, actually.'

'They're hardly a state secret!'

'Don't you believe me?'

'Should I?'

There was no mistaking Dane's tone now, and angered by it, Leslie stood up. 'I refuse to argue with you over nothing. I'm going to bed.'

She went to walk past him, but he caught her arm and swung her round to face him.

'I don't consider being made a fool of in my own home nothing,' he grated.

'I wasn't making a fool of you,' Leslie fumed. 'You're making a fool of yourself! Hal and I were

simply talking, not making it with each other.'
Recollecting the part she was supposed to be playing,
she battened down her anger and softened her voice.
'You know how I feel about you, darling, How could
you think I'd bear another man to touch me?'

'*Another* man?' Dane questioned. 'Don't you mean
any man?'

'What's that supposed to mean?'

'It means it's eight weeks since we made love,' he
snapped. 'You may not mind living like a nun, but I
sure as hell hate living like a monk!'

So that was it! It was all Leslie could do not to laugh.
'It won't be for much longer, darling.' she soothed.
'The doctor thinks I'll be fine in a couple of weeks.'
Deliberately she held out hope without making any
firm promise. After all, how could she when she didn't
know what her next move was going to be?

'Forgive me, sweetheart.' Shamefacedly Dane removed his hand from her arm. 'You can't help not
being well, and I'm a swine for forgetting it. It's just
that . . . well, you looked so beautiful tonight, I guess
my frustration got the better of me.'

'I'm frustrated too,' she said huskily, wishing with
all her heart that she wasn't. 'These past two months
have seemed like an eternity.'

With an inarticulate murmur, Dane drew her close
and wrapped his arms around her. 'I'm sorry for what
I said about you and Hal. I trust you implicitly,
sweetheart, and I always will.' He nuzzled her hair.
'You're the most honest woman I know.'

Guilt swamped her, and it took every ounce of her
willpower not to end this whole subterfuge. Yet the
memory of her beloved stepfather couldn't be ban-
ished, and her resolve hardened. Keeping her head on
Dane's chest, for in that way she could avoid his eyes,

which made it easier to lie to him, she said, 'You've been the most patient man, darling. You've never made me feel I've neglected you or——'

'Hey,' he cut in, 'you haven't neglected me. It's not your fault you haven't been well.'

'I know. But you've been so understanding.'

'The perfect husband, in fact,' he said drily. 'Now watch me prove it.' He tilted her face up to his, and kissed her softly on the mouth. 'Off to bed with you—before I forget the paragon I'm supposed to be!'

Leslie was still mulling over his words as dawn streaked the sky—she had never had so many sleepless nights in her life! Tonight had shown her that Dane's patience was wearing thin, and she wouldn't be one whit surprised if he suggested she consult another doctor. Worse still, he might insist on coming with her!

The thought of resuming their sexual life scared her, for it would lessen the control she was holding over her emotions, and once her control went, heaven knew where those emotions would lead her.

Only one solution remained: to end her marriage as quickly as possible. But what grounds could she give? She could hardly cite cruelty when Dane had been the kindest of men with her.

One idea after another surfaced in her mind, only to be discarded as impractical, too drastic, or plain heartless. Yet why should she worry about being heartless when it was Dane's cruelty to Robert that had prompted her to marry him in the first place? Was she going soft on him, or had the story she heard from Hal shown him to be more a traumatised man than an ogre?

Sighing heavily, she punched her pillow and lay back on it. She needed anger as an impetus to carry on with her scheme, yet at this moment she felt only compassion for Dane, a compassion that might grow into something far more disturbing if she stayed with him much longer.

CHAPTER THIRTEEN

LESLIE realised how much her feelings for Dane were changing as, later that morning, she watched him tuck into a hearty breakfast, after his early morning jog.

Today he seemed to have pushed himself extra hard—probably to rid himself of sexual frustration, she thought wryly—for though he had showered and changed from track-suit to light grey flannel, his cheeks were still flushed from exercise. He exuded health and vitality, and beside him she felt lifeless.

Ever observant, he commented on it as she sat down—though he couched it diplomatically.

'You look as if you've had a bad night, darling.'

'Just a headache,' she lied.

'Why not stay a few extra days with your cousins?'

'I've a site inspection first thing Monday, so I have to come back Sunday night.'

'Can't you switch it?' Warm brown eyes met aquamarine ones across the table. 'The break will do you good.'

'You're right. I'll come back Tuesday.' On an impulse, Leslie gave in. A few days away from Dane might help her get back her perspective. Certainly she couldn't carry on vacillating like this.

'I'm only sorry I can't join you,' he went on. 'But I'll be tied up all weekend with a client, and I can't put him off.'

'A *him*?' Leslie didn't hide her surpise. 'That's a turn-up for the books!'

'I thought you'd say that! Truth to tell, divorce is

154

beginning to bore me—which is why I went to see Dick Halsey a while back.' Dane referred to the District Attorney. 'I told him I was thinking of switching to criminal law, and he asked me to defend a friend of his, who's up on a corruption charge.' He replaced his napkin in its ivory holder. 'Remember our conversation on the way to Caldwell's party, soon after we got engaged?'

Leslie cast her mind back. 'When you said you'd changed your mind about a lot of things, but wouldn't be more specific?'

'So you do remember?' he chuckled. 'Well, now you know what I was referring to. Initially, I'd thought of changing course to please you, but then I found myself liking the idea more and more.'

So her criticism had sunk in!

'Does this mean you're giving up divorce work entirely?' she asked.

He rose and came round the table to her, tilting her face up to his. 'Sorry sweetheart, but no. It just means I'm widening my horizons.' He bent and pressed his mouth to the velvety skin of her throat. 'I'll call you at La Costa tonight. Miss me.'

The request had been unnecessary, for during the weekend Leslie felt so close to him it was impossible to regain her perspective of him.

'If you don't stop staring hopefully at the door every time a man comes through it, I'll scream!' Marybeth pronounced on the Saturday evening, over pre-dinner drinks.

Leslie sighed. 'It's silly of me, I know, but I ... Well, I thought Dane might surprise me by coming down.'

'But you said he was tied up with a client,' stated

Jack, ever practical. 'You're acting like a teenager with a crush, not an old married lady!'

'That's because she's a married lady with a crush!' Marybeth laughed, giving Leslie's arm an affectionate pat. 'Your face melts whenever you mention that husband of yours. I've never seen anyone so in love. I'm really happy for you, darling.'

The blood drained from Leslie's head as she realised Marybeth had said it all! Had voiced the thought she herself had refused to let surface because of her obsession with revenge.

She loved Dane!

She had probably loved him from the very beginning. But, embalmed in her bitterness, she had seen his ability to arouse her as a purely sexual response, rather than an emotionally caring one. And care for him she did, with every fibre of her being.

All at once so many other things she hadn't been able to understand fell into place: her changeable moods with him, her reluctance to look for a reason to divorce him. Oh God! How blind she had been not to see what he meant to her.

As her newly recognised emotions welled up, she experienced such a rush of joy she was alight with it, so alight that she could see things clearly for the first time in a year. Dane wasn't to blame for her stepfather's stroke. Robert had brought it on by his own stupidity in not recognising Charlene for what she was! Nothing could take away her love for the man who had helped bring her up, but she could finally accept that he had been the victim of his own folly.

With this acknowledgement came a deep sense of relief—and an urgency to confess everything to Dane. She knew he might not forgive her deception, and could well despise her for trapping him into marriage.

But it was a risk she had to take, for she could not contemplate a future with him based on lies.

'I must leave right away,' she blurted out, uncaring what her cousins thought of her sudden departure.

'Leave for where?' asked Jack, bewildered.

'Los Angeles.'

'But you promised to spend the week with us,' Marybeth reproached.

'I know. but I've just discovered something wonderful and I have to tell Dane. It's all *your* doing, Marybeth!'

'Mine?'

'Yes, you! You've made me realise I'm crazily, wildly, madly in love with my husband! And I can't wait to tell him.'

'You're not making sense,' Jack said blankly.

'Yes, I am,' Leslie bubbled, jumping to her feet, her excited glance encompassing them both. 'Bear with me, will you, darlings? I'll tell you the whole story as soon as I can. But I have to see Dane first.'

Within half an hour she was packed and on her way home, her foot hard down on the accelerator. Normally a careful driver, she ignored the speed limit and watched the needle touch seventy, only her fear of a blow-out preventing her going even faster.

It was almost midnight when she turned into the basement parking below the penthouse. As she did, her headlights beamed on the elevator doors slowly opening, and, surprised, she saw the tall broad-shouldered figure of her husband step out.

But he was not alone. A strikingly pretty brunette emerged with him, and with anguished horror Leslie saw the girl smile into his face, and Dane bend and gently stroke her cheek.

Heart racing like a piston, yet brain ice-cold, Leslie

swerved into the furthest parking bay, praying he hadn't seen her. Yet why should he when his eyes were riveted on his companion?

There was no doubting the tenderness between them, and Leslie felt as if her breath was being squeezed from her chest by a vice of pain. She might have found the agony easier to bear if she could make herself believe this was nothing other than a chance pick-up, but the look on Dane's face, the tender movements of his hands on the girl's cheek and hair, smacked of friendship renewed—or worse still, of a friendship that had never been severed.

Recalling his recent trip to New York, and his occasional nights away from home, ostensibly on business, Leslie writhed at her naïvety. She had believed that despite their not going to bed together, he had remained faithful to her, had even thought he was falling in love with her!

The realisation that she had been fooling herself was almost more than she could bear, and long after Dane's Porsche had roared away into the night, she went on staring blindly through the windscreen at the brick wall facing her. Jealousy, anger, hurt, melded into deep sadness as she visualised him in the other girl's arms: kissing her, holding her, touching her intimately.

Her sadness deepened as she mourned for a love so recently found and so suddenly lost. Whose fault it was was unimportant. All she knew was that she could not live with a man who was incapable of commitment to one woman.

When she finally managed to pull herself together, she went up to the penthouse and packed her clothes, leaving behind everything Dane had given her. Then she carried the cases down to her car and locked them in her boot.

She wanted to rush away that instant, never to see or speak to Dane again, but pride wouldn't let her, and she returned to the penthouse, freshened her make-up and went into the living-room.

Barely had she settled on the settee when she heard Dane's steps on the marble-floored hall. Drawing on all her inner strength, Leslie forced herself to stay where she was, her features carefully composed as he came in.

His astonishment at seeing her on one of the long, velvet couches would have been ludicrous had she not known that guilt, rather than pleasure, lay behind it, and it was all she could do not to hurl accusations at him like a harridan. But she could hurt him more by toying with him for a while, as he so often did with his victims in court.

'Darling!' He came striding across to her. 'Why are you home? Nothing wrong, I hope?'

'Only that I missed you too much to stay away!' She managed a starry-eyed look. 'Did you miss *me*?'

'Goes without saying.' He reached out to pull her up, but she retreated further into the cushions and glanced at her watch.

'Quite a session you had with your client,' she murmured. 'It's almost two o'clock.'

Dane looked momentarily discomfited. 'We didn't finish in the office till around ten, and then I took him to Spago's for dinner.' He named a restaurant frequented by the movie colony. 'You know what a lively place it is, and I thought it might take his mind off his problems.'

'I thought Spago's was closed on Sundays?' she questioned innocently.

Dane swallowed hard, visibly shaken by his gaffe. 'So it is. I meant The Carnival.'

'They don't sound a bit alike,' she chided. 'How come you made such a mistake?'

'Guess I'm tired,' he excused himself lamely.

'But not from work!' she flung at him, her control snapping. 'I damn well saw you come out of the elevator at midnight with your girl-friend!'

Dane's indrawn breath was audible, but Leslie could see no sign of guilt. The opposite, in fact, for his jaw jutted forward aggressively.

'Is that why you came back earlier than planned?' he demanded. 'So you could spy on me?' Astonishingly he was now the accuser, not the defendant.

Until this moment, Leslie had had no intention of confessing everything. She had planned to continue acting the wronged wife, and leave with the burden of guilt resting firmly on Dane's shoulders, but the urge to make him suffer was too strong, and she lashed out at him furiously.

'How clever of you to guess! I knew from the start you were incapable of being faithful to one woman. So it was simply a matter of staying with you until I could find grounds for divorce!'

'You mean you've been *looking* for grounds?' He was so flummoxed he fell silent, his puzzled expression showing he didn't grasp the implication of what she had said. 'Are you telling me you married me with the sole intention of divorcing me?'

'Yes!'

'But why? For God's sake why?'

Because Robert Jordan—Charlene Jordan's husband, in case you've forgotten—was my stepfather.'

Slowly the colour ebbed from Dane's face, and his tan took on a yellowish tinge.

'I was in court the day you practically destroyed him,' she went on relentlessly. 'I watched you strip away his pride and make him a laughing-stock. And if that wasn't enough, you made sure Charlene sold the shares he'd given her to his biggest rival—which was the most despicable thing of all!'

Dane's mouth narrowed with temper. 'She told you, I suppose?'

'Yes. She came specially to Robert's funeral to do so.' Hope flared in Leslie and she could not stop herself voicing it. 'Isn't it true then? *Didn't* you make her sell to Imtex?'

'Trying to find something good in me?' Dane sneered. 'Don't waste your time, sweetheart; I told her exactly what to do.'

Bitterness rose like gall in Leslie's throat. 'I don't know how you can sleep easy at night knowing you caused a man's death. Robert would never have had a stroke if it hadn't been for you!'

Although Leslie no longer believed this, it was the way she had felt when she had married Dane, and she wanted him to know it.

'You really do hate me, don't you?' he said thickly.

'You'll never know how much,' she lied, an image of the black-haired girl rising before her. 'And tonight you played right into my hands. I'm going to divorce you for adultery and get the biggest alimony California's ever seen!'

'I'll deny it,' he told her.

'I've other grounds too.'

'Such as?'

'Mental cruelty; making my life a misery I couldn't bear going to bed with you. I even showed my doctor the bruises I got when you tried to force yourself on me.'

Dane's mouth went slack. 'Bruises? How in hell could you get bruises when I never laid a hand on you?'

'I fell climbing a ladder,' she confessed, 'and the black and blue marks on my shoulder were too good to waste.'

'You scheming bitch!' he grated. 'I've met a few in my time, but you're the worst!'

'Pity you didn't realise it before,' she taunted. 'What a story it'll make when it hits the papers! Brilliant lawyer played for a fool by the very sort of woman he's always defended!'

Silently Dane stared at her. His face was expressionless, and Leslie felt she was looking at a statue. Yet she knew him well enough to sense he was deeply shocked by her disclosures, so shocked that he was exerting iron control not to give her the satisfaction of seeing it. But she felt no sympathy for him; only anger against herself for thinking their marriage could have worked.

Silently she walked into the hall and pressed the elevator button, conscious of Dane's eyes boring into her.

'Goodbye,' she said loftily. 'See you in court.'

'I won't give you that pleasure,' he shot back. 'I'll settle out of it.'

'How intelligent of you. At least you'll save face—if not money!'

'My motive's purely altruistic,' he answered. 'I'd be prepared to give everything I owned never to set eyes on you again!'

'I'd never take *everything*,' she said sweetly. 'I'll leave you enough to keep your girl-friends in the manner to which you're accustomed!'

He strode towards the elevator, and Leslie flinched

back inside it, positive he was going to strike her. But she was wrong. All he did was press the button to close the door, as though the sight of her was more than he could bear.

CHAPTER FOURTEEN

LESLIE'S inclination, following her separation from Dane, was to leave her job and settle in another city, where there would be no reminders of him, no remembrance of their brief span together.

But she was loath to give up her job, and when she was unexpectedly offered a full partnership she couldn't bring herself to refuse it. However, she handed over the completion of Dane's house to one of the other architects in her firm.

Fortunately, she had retained the lease on her own apartment—though she had told Dane she had sublet it—and was able to move back straight away. Her 'daily' had kept the rooms spick and span, and once her clothes were back in the cupboards it was as if she had never been away. Well, almost, she admitted sadly to herself in the dark reaches of the night, for she was no longer the same person who had once lived here.

Her threat to sue Dane for every cent she could had been an empty one, for now she had re-assessed her stepfather's behaviour, she couldn't in all conscience hold Dane accountable for it. She still condemned him for the way he had behaved over Charlene's shares, but knew that seeking retribution would only give her a Pyrrhic victory. Love—at least for her—did not go hand in hand with vengeance.

To this end she instructed her attorney not even to ask for maintenance, a decision both he and her friends considered crazy. But to make Dane pay for being unfaithful to her—which was the reason she had given for the breakdown of their marriage—would have made her as grasping as the women he himself represented in court.

She often wondered what Dane had made of her change of heart, but no gossip filtered back to her. Well, let him think what he liked. She was the one who had to live with her conscience, and she wanted no regrets to cloud her future.

As the weeks stretched into months, she began dating other men, and appreciated how irrevocable her love for Dane was. Never again would she find the same *joie de vivre* with anyone, the same excitement and contentment, passion and serenity.

Work was her panacea and she flung herself into it. Her diary was full for weeks ahead, wih so many assignments out of town that her partners laughingly began calling her the firm's 'roving ambassadress,' though beneath their humour was a genuine concern for her well-being.

'Time you took a break,' Ben McMallister, the most senior partner, said one afternoon, coming into her office. 'All work and no play is a recipe for disaster, not oblivion. I know you're going through a tough patch, Leslie, but a nervous breakdown isn't the solution. You should take a vacation. See new places and faces.'

Leslie sighed and set down her pen, knowing she couldn't ignore Ben's advice. 'I appreciate your concern, Ben, and I'll go away as soon as my divorce comes through—I promise. But until it has, I can't relax, and a vacation would be a total waste.'

'Well, that makes sense.' He ran a hand through his grizzled hair. 'But at least ease up on your workload, and that means no files in your briefcase when you leave on a Friday night!'

'That'll be a hard rule to obey,' Leslie said ruefully.

'Not this weekend, it won't. Lois and I want you to join us on our boat. I know how much you like sailing, and we'd love to have you.'

'And I'd love to accept,' Leslie said gratefully. She had not taken out her own boat since marrying Dane, and even though she was now alone she had lost heart to do so.

'We'll pick you up early Friday evening,' Ben went on. 'Lois will call and fix the time.'

Alone again, Leslie decided to grab a coffee and a sandwich before her next appointment. She wasn't hungry, but knew it was vital to keep up her energy.

As she munched smoked salmon on rye, her eye caught the band of paler skin on the third finger of her left hand, where her wedding ring had been. Of all the jewellery Dane had given her, it was the only item she regretted leaving, though why this should be so was a mystery, for it was as meaningless as everything else he had lavished on her, an empty gesture from an empty heart.

Miserably she wondered who Dane was seeing now. One thing was certain—he wasn't spending his spare time alone! Yet though she always glanced at the gossip columns to see who was the current recipient of his favours, the only news of him was professional. He had successfully defended the District Attorney's friend on a corruption charge, after a brilliant summation that had earned him the front covers of *Time* and *Newsweek*.

But his private life remained private, and even his move to his new house hadn't taken place in the blaze of publicity she had expected. Indeed, she had only learned of it from Beverly and Caldwell, with whom she remained on friendly terms after an initial but understandable coolness.

She was having dinner with them tonight, though she had first made sure Dane wouldn't be there.

'I know your instincts are to get us together again,' Leslie had told Beverly. 'But it's over and done with, and the sooner everyone accepts it, the better.'

'Such a waste,' the redhead had sighed. 'If ever two people seemed to have it made!'

The buzzer interrupted Leslie's reverie, and hastily finishing her coffee, she threw the plastic container into the bin, and composed herself to meet her client.

The woman who came in was above average height, with fashionably cut dark hair framing a beautifully made-up face that was as well preserved as the figure beneath the grey Ralph Lauren suit. From the doorway she looked little more than fifty, though as she drew nearer the lines on her face proclaimed her at least ten years older.

'Mrs Barrett?' Leslie rose to greet her, liking the smiling mouth and warm brown eyes. 'Do sit down.' She indicated a chair and took her own again. 'I gather you want some advice on a property conversion?'

'Yes, I do.' The woman's voice was as pleasing to the ear as her appearance to the eye. 'I've been doing it as a hobby for years, but have finally decided to turn professional.'

'Be careful you don't turn a hobby into a headache!'

'That's why I've come to you! I hope you aren't too busy to take me on?'

Although she had more than enough work to cope with, Leslie shook her head. She had never had any dealings with a woman property developer and rather fancied the idea.

'Tell me exactly what you have in mind,' she said. 'I

assume you have some houses for me to see?'

'Five, actually. I'm sure two of them will do fine, but I'd appreciate your opinion on the others.'

'That's a day's work at least.' Leslie glanced at her diary. 'I'm afraid I can't do it before Friday.'

'Oh dear,' Mrs Barrett sighed. 'I'm leaving on that day. I don't live here, you see, and I was hoping to get my lawyer cracking on the contracts before I go.'

'Hm, that's tricky, then. Look, I'll see if my secretary can switch around my appointments for tomorrow.'

Briefly Leslie spoke into the intercom, then, while she waited to see if her meetings could be rearranged. Mrs Barrett filled her in on the type of conversions she did, which was turning big old houses into one-room studio apartments.

'How many conversions have you done so far?' Leslie asked.

'About twelve.'

'Some hobby! What decided you to look in L.A.?'

'I've a son here, and it will give me an excuse to see him more often! I might even move here, if things work out.'

Leslie felt Mrs Barrett would *make* things work out for her. There was a strength about the woman that appealed, and a no-nonsense attitude that didn't go with the fashion-plate appearance. All in all she could be a most interesting client.

'I've managed to switch all tomorrow's appointments to Friday,' her secretary popped her head round the door to say.

'Clever girl,' Leslie approved, and glanced at Mrs Barrett. 'If we've five houses to see, we'd better make an early start.'

'You wouldn't be free some time today?'

'That's pushing your luck!' Leslie grinned. 'Let's make it nine tomorrow. If you can tell me where to meet you ...'

No sooner had the woman gone than Leslie headed downtown to see a boxing promoter who wished to put up a leisure centre. Seven other people were providing the finance and there were seven egos to be massaged, so that by the time she reached home she was mentally drained.

A leisurely soak in a warm bath revived her sufficiently to look forward to the evening ahead, and with some of her old verve, she searched among her clothes for her prettiest dress, wound her long streaky blonde hair into an elaborate coil atop her head, and set off for Bel Air.

Unlike most of Caldwell's parties, this one was informal, and she was delighted to find she knew several of the guests, though sight of Hal, Dane's accountant, was momentarily off-putting. Not for him though, for he strode over to her with a beaming smile.

'Long time no see, Leslie. You look beautiful as ever.'

She knew he was exaggerating, for her mirror—to say nothing of her partner Ben—had confirmed she was too drawn-looking, her green eyes too large in a face shadowed by lack of sleep.

'You look pretty good yourself,' she replied, and saw his eyes dart to a small, plump young woman talking to Caldwell. 'Number four?' she questioned softly.

He nodded happily. 'She's a psychiatrist in Santa Monica. With the alimony I'm paying out, I figured it was better to marry a shrink than to visit one!'

Leslie laughed, and from the fatuous look on Hal's face, knew he was being deliberately facetious.

'But enough about me,' he went on, grabbing two

glasses of champagne from a passing tray, and handing her one. 'What's with you?'

'I've been made a full partner and have a loo of my very own!'

'Wow! You really are in the big time.' He patted her arm affectionately. 'But I wasn't thinking in professional terms. I'm more interested in knowing if there's a chance of you and Dane getting back together. I think you're wrong to break up a good marriage because of one little mistake.'

'One little mistake wouldn't,' she said gently. 'But when your husband makes it with another woman after only five months . . .'

For a fleeting instant Hal could not hide his discomfiture. 'I'm sure there's an explanation.'

'Has Dane given you one?'

'He refuses to discuss it. But——'

'And so do I,' Leslie cut in, weary of yet another well-intentioned interferer. 'We married for the wrong reasons, Hal, and it's better we end it.'

Perilously close to tears, she went quickly from the room, longing for the security of her own apartment, yet determined not to run away.

'Hal doing the best-friend act, I suppose?' Beverly grumbled, hurrying into the powder-room after her.

'He means well.' Leslie dabbed at her eyes with a tissue. 'I'll be fine in a minute.'

'Take as long as you like, honey. I'll hold back dinner.'

'And ruin it?' Leslie questioned ruefully. 'You told me the menu, dear friend, and there's no way lobster soufflés can wait!'

'Sure they can. No one here tonight's a gourmet, and if the soufflés go flat, I'll tell them they're lobster pancakes!'

Laughing through her tears, Leslie linked her arm through Beverly's as they returned to the living-room.

It was well past midnight before she was home, feeling far more light-headed than when she had left. Yet the instant she walked into the bedroom she remembered the one she had shared with Dane on their honeymoon, and the tender expertise with which he had initiated her into the art of love; careful not to shock her, not to ask her to do more than she wanted, but gently showing her, with his hands and tongue, how they could please each other. Her limbs trembled at the memories that came flooding back, and she sank on to the bed and buried her head in her hands.

Predictably, her sleep was broken by vivid dreams of him, and she was heavy-eyed and in no mood for seeing the lively Mrs Barrett when she stepped from her car outside the clapboard house in Brentwood that was their meeting-place.

A quick view told Leslie the property was a disaster, and they drove the three blocks to the next one. This proved a better proposition, as did the remaining houses, and the rest of the day was spent meticulously examining them.

It was six o'clock before they were finally finished, and Mrs Barrett took the passenger seat in Leslie's car.

'It's going to be a big undertaking for you to supervise,' she said 'and I'd like to give you a profit participation in the scheme.'

Though gratified by the compliment, Leslie shook her head. 'That's very generous of you, Mrs Barrett, but it isn't necessary, and anyway, I couldn't accept.'

'Why not?'

'Because I feel . . . well, let's just say I'll give this job my full attention whether I share in the profits or not, so there's no need for you to offer me an incentive.'

'But I want to.'

'The answer's still no—but thanks.'

'Are you always this obstinate?'

'Where my ethics are concerned.' Leslie pulled a face. 'Now I sound a real moralising prig, don't I?'

'On the contrary. But tell me, would you consider it a bribe if I asked you to dinner?'

'I'd consider it an act of kindness,' Leslie chuckled. 'I'm starving!' She pressed her foot harder on the accelerator. 'There's an excellent little restaurant around the corner from my office, where——'

'No round the corner little restaurant for us,' Mrs Barrett interrupted. 'It's the Beverly Hills Hotel or nothing!'

'I doubt we'll get a table there without booking ahead.'

'I made a reservation on the offchance.'

'How far-sighted of you!'

'Let's just say I was hopeful.'

An undertone in Mrs Barrett's voice made Leslie shoot her a sidelong glance, but it was met by a bland one that told her nothing.

'A drink in the Polo Lounge first,' the woman stated as they left the car to be parked by an attendant. 'Then a leisurely meal—if you won't be bored.'

'Why should I be?' asked Leslie, surprised.

'At dining with a woman. A pretty young thing like you must be turning men away.'

'At the moment I'm not dating anyone,' Leslie confessed.

'How come?'

'I'm in the process of getting divorced.'

Further conversation was forestalled by their being led to a table in the Polo Lounge, where Mrs Barrett ordered a half-bottle of champagne to celebrate her new business venture.

'It might be wiser to leave the celebrating till the end,' Leslie said drily. 'Conversions have a habit of developing unexpected snags, as I'm sure you know, and all the planning in the world can't foresee them.'

'Like marriage,' I suppose,' Mrs Barrett mused. 'A couple start off with the best of intentions and then find things don't work out.'

'That sounds like experience talking!'

'It is. I had a bitter divorce and it took me years to rebuild my life successfully.'

'It won't take *me* years,' Leslie said vehemently. 'I can't wait to be free.'

'How long were you married?'

'Only a few months. But if you know something isn't going to work it's best to end it.'

'Were you so unhappy, then?' asked Mrs Barrett.

Leslie shrugged for answer. Although she found the woman easy to talk to, she was reluctant, on such short acquaintance, to open her heart to her.

'I'm prying, I know,' Mrs Barrett admitted, 'but you're so intelligent and warm that——'

'It takes two to make a marriage,' Leslie put in. 'No matter how warm and intelligent one partner is, if the other *isn't* . . .'

'Now you really surprise me.'

'Why?'

'Because I can't see you marrying a man who didn't have these qualities.'

'We all make mistakes,' Leslie said lightly, 'but luckily I found out mine early on.' Raising her glass in mock salute to herself, she drained it and set it on the table.

Mrs Barrett did the same, then stood up. 'So much

easier to talk in the restaurant,' she murmured.
'Besides, if I drink any more without eating, I'll fall on
my face!'

The dining-room was three-quarters full, but they
were shown to an excellent table, an honour that made
Leslie wonder if Mrs Barrett's son was well known in
the movie business.

'Oh no,' came the reply, when Leslie ventured to
ask, as they were eating their way through a delicious
Chateaubriand, sliced in front of them and served on a
bed of organically grown vegetables. 'He's a lawyer, as
a matter of fact.'

The word 'lawyer' was like a stab in Leslie's heart,
and her fork clattered to her plate.

'Anything wrong?' Mrs Barrett enquired.

'N-no. Just that—that my husband's a lawyer too.'

'I know.'

'You *know*?'

'Yes, my dear. And I've a confession to make.
Barrett's my maiden name. My married name's
Jordan, and Dane is my son.'

A hot wave of anger swept over Leslie, and as
quickly receded, leaving her ice-cold.

'I'm sorry to hear that,' she managed to say. 'It
means we've both wasted our time today. Now if you'll
excuse me, I'll go.'

'Please don't—not yet at least. I know you're angry
with me, but I'm fighting for my son's happiness.'

'Did he send you?'

'Certainly not. In fact he'd be furious if he knew.
Now please, my dear, won't you hear me out?'

It was the last thing she wanted. Yet she found it
impossible to ignore Mrs Jordan's pleading, and even
as she hesitated the woman spoke again.

'All I'm asking for is five minutes of your time. If you want to leave after that, then so be it.'

CHAPTER FIFTEEN

LESLIE settled back in her chair and looked across the table at Mrs Jordan.

'I apologise again for meeting you under false pretences,' the woman said, 'but I couldn't think of any other way.'

'You could have called and told me who you were,' Leslie couldn't resist saying. 'I might have agreed to see you.'

'No, you wouldn't.' Mrs Jordan saw confirmation in Leslie's eyes and gave a wry smile. 'Now you know why I didn't! But I really am in the property business, Leslie, and I hope you'll work on my project regardless of what happens between you and my son.'

'That's impossible. It would be too painful.'

'Painful?' Mrs Jordan pounced on the word. 'Then you still care for him?'

'I didn't say that!'

'Then why should it be painful to see me? You were married such a short while, it shouldn't take you long to forget the whole episode.'

'I find any kind of failure painful,' Leslie said, awarding Mrs Jordan marks for perception.

'In that case, I'm surprised you didn't fight for your marriage.'

'It wasn't worth saving.' Trembling with angry remembrance of Dane emerging from the elevator with another woman, Leslie picked up her purse. 'Look, much as I'd have enjoyed working with you, I don't see any point continuing this discussion.'

'But you promised to hear me out! I'm fighting for my son's happiness, Leslie, and even if I fail, I'd like to have the satisfaction of knowing I tried.'

'Do you know the whole story?'

'I know enough to appreciate why you walked out, but——'

'There's more to it than that,' Leslie intervened, and though reluctant to talk about her stepfather, felt Mrs Jordan had a right to hear part of the story at least.

In a voice as controlled as her expression, she recounted the bare facts about Robert and Charlene, and explained why she had deliberately set out to marry Dane; then briefly touched on why *he* had married *her*.

'I've never heard two more immature reasons for getting married' came the comment. 'Sex and vengeance—really! I'd like to bang both your silly heads together!'

Leslie lowered her eyes. 'We were both wrong, and we've both paid the price.'

'My son certainly has. I've never seen him so unhappy.'

'Only because he's lost face. I mean a divorce lawyer being divorced after a few months' marriage!'

'His pride has nothing to do with it. He cares for you, Leslie. I don't know if it's love—he refuses to discuss you—but I do know you mean more to him than any girl he's known.'

'No matter how many times you multiply nothing you still get nothing!' Leslie retorted. 'On his own admission, Dane's never loved any woman, apart from you, that is. He's had affairs, but he's always run a mile from a caring relationship.'

'In the past, maybe, but I'm sure that isn't the case today.'

'I'd find that easier to credit if he hadn't committed adultery,' Leslie said bitterly. 'In fact the only decent thing he did was not play me for a fool by denying it.'

'Then that's *something* in his favour,' Mrs Jordan rejoined. 'Which is more than you can say about yourself! You lied to him from the word go!'

Remembering the dishonest ploys she had used to get Dane to propose, Leslie could not defend herself. Yet that didn't make his adultery any the easier to forgive.

'My marrying Dane was wrong,' she admitted, 'but I'm right to end it. I can't be happy with a man who's incapable of being faithful to me for more than a few months!'

'Then you *do* care for him!'

'Yes, dammit, I do! But I'm still going ahead with the divorce. Now if you'll excuse me . . .'

Leslie went to rise, but was stayed by a surprisingly firm hand.

'Will you let me make one more comment, my dear?' Leslie nodded stonily, and Mrs Jordan went on, 'Have you considered the possibility that Dane guessed you didn't love him when you married him?'

'No. I put on a marvellous act.'

'He may still have been subconsciously aware of it.'

'What are you trying to prove?' asked Leslie.

'Whether that's the reason why he turned to someone else. Men often do when their pride is hurt. Not commendable, I know, but—well, look what pride has made *you* do. It stopped you telling him you had a change of heart regarding your stepfather, and made you walk out on a man you love, instead of overlooking an act of infidelity for which I think you were partly to blame!'

This was turning the tables with a vengeance, and

much as Leslie longed to counter it, honesty wouldn't let her. Intuition could well have made Dane suspect her feelings, and his doubts would have grown when he had found himself relegated to the dressing-room, and shortly afterwards barred from her bed. But this didn't make his adultery less reprehensible.

'All this talk is getting us nowhere,' she said. 'I'll never forgive Dane.'

'I know that's how you feel at the moment, my dear. But what about next year, or the year after?'

'I'll still feel the same.'

'Then I pity you. Living with bitterness will sour your life.' The older woman's mouth moved tremulously. '*I* had to live with bitterness for years because there was nothing I could do to eradicate it. But *you* can.'

'How?'

'By seeing Dane and admitting you were equally culpable for what's happened.'

'I can't say that.'

'Why not? It's the truth! My son at least started his marriage with honesty, which is more than you can say for yourself!'

Leslie flinched. 'You hit hard, don't you?'

'I'll hit harder if need be. I'm fighting for his happiness.'

'What makes you think he'll find it with me?'

'Because he married you! Regardless of the reason he gave for doing so, I think that deep down he felt quite differently about you from how he did about previous girl-friends, though he probably didn't realise it until he'd actually made you his wife.'

'You're a great publicist for him,' muttered Leslie.

'I'm simply stating the situation as I see it.' Mrs Jordan abruptly signalled for the bill. 'If you disagree with me, then the quicker you divorce him and get back to square one the better.'

Leslie sighed heavily. She didn't have a snowball's chance in hell of getting back to square one. What she felt for Dane would colour the rest of her life. That being the case, wasn't it better to swallow her pride and see if they could begin again?

'All right,' she said huskily. 'You win. I'll go and see him.'

'Thank goodness for that! Well, go on, girl! What are you waiting for?'

'I can't go tonight,' Leslie panicked. 'I need more time. Maybe tomorrow. Anyway, he mightn't be in.'

'He is. He's waiting to take me to dinner, in fact.'

Leslie drew a shaky breath. 'I bet you planned all this.'

'Let's say I had hopes. Now no more talking. *Go and see him!*'

Pausing only to give Mrs Jordan a tearful smile, Leslie ran from the restaurant.

Luckily the drive to the penthouse was a short one, or she might have lost her nerve and gone home. Indeed, as the block came in sight, she had to battle with the urge to leave things as they were, to accept the sleepless nights, the loneliness, the anguished 'might have beens'. A shudder ripped through her at the very idea of such a future, and she knew she would do anything rather than face that. If Dane cared for her, as his mother said, and if she could actually get him to admit it, they might stand a chance of being successful the second time around.

She kept this thought firmly in mind as she took the private elevator to the top floor, and a front door she had never expected to see again. Not giving herself pause for thought, she pressed the bell and kept her finger there.

'OK, OK,' a deep voice called, 'I'm coming!'

On the last word the door flew open and Leslie found herself staring at Dane. How thin he was, his eyes shadowed, deep hollows beneath the cheekbones! If the past few months had not dealt kindly with her, they had been even less kind to him, and she was overwhelmed by a longing to pull him close and smooth away the lines; to assure him that no matter what, she was here and would never leave him.

'I love you,' she said baldly, 'I think I always have.'

The words came from her of their own volition, and she could no more have held them back than Niagara could have stayed its waters.

Dane gave a slight shake of his head, as if testing his hearing. 'That's not what you led me to believe the night you walked out on me,' he said in the polite tone of a stranger.

'I was angry and jealous and wanted to hurt you.'

'And you're no longer angry and jealous?'

'I didn't say that! But I see now that hurting you hurt me even more!'

'Even more than what?'

'Don't p-play word games with me,' Leslie said jerkily. 'I-I know how I feel about you, but I've n-no idea what you feel for me.'

'Right now I feel I'd like to shut the door on you!'

Shocked, she stared at him, and was on the verge of turning away when she noticed the tremor in the hand still gripping the edge of the door.

'What's stopping you?' she asked.

'Good manners, curiosity—yes, predominantly curiosity.'

Abruptly he turned and went into the living-room,

not asking her to follow, not even looking round to see if she did.

Trembling, she did so, emotion gripping her as she entered the white and beige interior, saw the delicate fruit-drop colours of the velvet settees, the shining radiance of the white and gold marble floor, the jewel tones of the silk rugs. Nothing had changed, She could almost believe she had been here yesterday.

Only Dane looked different: a stranger almost, in a navy suit of finest mohair, its impeccable cut not quite managing to hide that he had lost a great deal of weight. Not that it detracted from his sensuality, her racing pulses signalled, for the haggard, brooding moodiness on his face awakened her desire.

'Well now,' he began, turning from the window to regard her. 'What caused your change of heart?'

'I met your mother,' Leslie said simply.

His muttered imprecation took her unawares, for he was not a man given to swearing.

'Don't blame her,' she said quickly. 'She wanted to see me, and came to my office as a client.'

'Good God!' There was enlightenment in the exclamation. 'What did she say to you to bring you here?'

'She—she convinced me I was as much to blame as you for what happened.'

'My infidelity, you mean?'

Leslie swallowed painfully. 'Yes.'

'I suppose she said I went roving because I sensed you didn't love me?'

His voice was as coolly uninterested as though they were discussing the weather, and Leslie flung him a startled glance.

'No, she didn't say the same to me,' he added. 'But only because I refused to discuss my marriage with her. However, she obviously said it to you.'

'Yes, she did.'

'And that makes you willing to forgive me?'

'I think we should forgive each other.'

Leslie moved a step closer, and felt rather than saw him draw back. Only then did it dawn on her he might not want her; that regardless of what Mrs Jordan had said, he wanted to rebuild his life without her. Despair rooted her to the spot. It wouldn't be the first time a mother had misunderstood her son's motives.

'I'm s—sorry if I've embarrassed you by coming here,' she stammered. 'It seemed like a g-good idea at the time.'

Blindly she turned, and was halfway across the room when his voice stopped her.

'The thing is, would you really be able to forget Gail?'

So that was her name! Leslie clenched her hands so tightly her nails dug into the soft skin of her palms. It wasn't only a matter of forgetting Gail, but of whether she could forgive Dane.

'Yes,' she said faintly, answering his spoken question and her own silent one. 'Yes, I can,' she repeated, keeping her back to him so that he wouldn't see the anguish in her face. 'But only if you help me, Dane. I don't want the sort of marriage we had before, where I feel you only want me sexually. If you still won't allow yourself to love me, then it's better we leave things as they are.'

There was a lengthy silence and Leslie turned slowly. Dane was watching her, his eyes brooding, his brows drawn together above them.

'There's no question of "allowing myself to love you",' he said flatly.

Leslie felt as though her life-force was draining

away. The room blurred, and with an enormous effort she retained control of her senses.

'Thank you for being honest with me, Dane.'

Not trusting herself to continue, she made for the door, startled when he was suddenly in front of her, so close she could feel the warmth radiating from his body.

'You misunderstand me, Leslie. How can I allow myself to fall in love when I'm *already* in love?'

She stared at him, afraid to believe what he was saying.

'I saw what love did to my mother when my father walked out on her,' he went on huskily, 'and I vowed I'd never let it happen to me. That's why I always had to be in control of my emotions. And then I met you and you turned my world upside down! But I wouldn't admit it. I kidded myself that my need for you was only physical; that I wanted you with my body, not my heart.' He gave a harsh laugh. 'Shows what a fool I was! On the first night of our honeymoon I'd have lain on the floor and let you walk over me. In fact I damn well did! I suppose keeping me out of your bed was the first step on the road you'd planned for me?'

Shamefacedly she nodded. 'I wish I could turn back the clock.'

'I don't,' he said unexpectedly. 'It took your walking out on me to make me admit how I felt about you.'

Though overjoyed to hear this, Leslie found the words bitter-sweet, for turning back the clock would have meant no Gail, no images of Dane with another woman, his passion assuaged by someone other than herself.

'I know what's going through your mind, sweetheart,' he murmured, 'but you can forget it. Gail never was—and there never has been!'

Leslie stared into his eyes. 'Never has been?'

'Another woman. Not since the day you agreed to marry me.'

'But Gail——'

'Was my secretary until two years ago, when she went to live in Carmel with her boy-friend.'

'Your secretary!'

'*Only*,' he emphasised. 'Six months ago she discovered Johnny was into drugs, and moved back to L.A. But he kept pestering her to return to him, and when she wouldn't, he started beating her up. The night you came back from La Costa—when I was meant to be seeing a client—Gail called and said she and Johnny had had another fight and she'd knocked him out with a lampstand. She was petrified she'd killed him and I went straight over to see her. Luckily he was only concussed, and we got him to hospital and then went on to the police to make a statement. After that, I brought her here to calm her down. When you saw us, I was taking her home.'

'Why didn't you tell me all this before?' Leslie whispered. 'Why did you let me think the worst of you?'

'Because I was furious at your stupidity. I thought I'd made it so clear I was crazy about you, I couldn't believe you'd think I'd *look* at another woman, let alone go to bed with one! Oh, sweetheart,' he murmured unsteadily, 'don't you know you're the only one for me? That I love you to distraction and want to spend the rest of my life showing you how much?'

'If only you'd said it!' cried Leslie, touching her hands to his cheek, his mouth, the pulse beating erratically in his throat.

'I couldn't bring myself to,' he confessed, drawing her close to his body, his hands moving down her spine to cup her buttocks gently and press them closer to his thighs. 'I thought I'd shown you in so many other ways.'

Even as he spoke, she knew there was something else he hadn't been able to bring himself to say, and she put her hands on his shoulders and pulled slightly away from him, so that she could look into his face.

'If you let me believe the worst with Gail, would I be right in assuming you did the same over Charlene's shares?'

He did not answer, but the burning glow in his eyes gave him away.

'You didn't make her sell to Imtex, did you?' Leslie stated.

'No. She did the deal without even telling me. I know I stung your stepfather over alimony, but I'd never have destroyed his business.'

'You should have told me!' Leslie cried.

'I wanted you to show some faith in me. And it hurt like hell when you didn't.'

'We both have such a lot to learn,' she sighed.

'So it seems. I'm going to make a tape recording of my feelings and play it in every room on the hour!'

'There are other ways you can show me,' Leslie teased.

'At the moment I can think of only one!'

'Me too!'

She unbuttoned his jacket and placed her hands on his chest, feeling the warmth of his body through his silk shirt. As her hand slipped lower, he trembled, then brought his mouth down on hers, his tongue hot and demanding, thrusting forward aggressively as passion rose high.

Sensuously Leslie rubbed her body against his, her breasts hardening as she felt his swelling arousal. Her